Damien To...
Or...
And ...

She glided with c... ...,
setting guest lists on tables. She smiled at the wait
staff in a friendlier, more open way than she did
him. That fact stuck in his craw. He wondered
what it would be like if she were that open with
him. He felt an odd wrench in his gut and watched
her through eyes lowered to half-mast. Why
should it bother him?

He would have her. In every way a man could
have a woman, he was determined to have her, and
he would.

Damien took another swallow of whiskey and
felt the burn all the way down. Not only would
she give him herself, she would give him all the
information he wanted to make Max De Luca pay.

Dear Reader,

What could be better than a billionaire who is tamed by an everyday woman like you and me? A man driven to succeed and take his revenge against those who have made his family suffer. A man who succeeded against the odds who needs to be saved from his bitterness and vengefulness.

Maybe a woman like you or me could teach him to love and be loved.

Now, that would take a miracle—the miracle of love. You and I know about this miracle. It's the best one of all.

I'm so pleased to present *Billionaire Extraordinaire* to you—the story of a scarred man who needs to learn how to love and the woman who teaches him, despite her most sensible efforts to resist him.

Billionaire Extraordinaire marks the publication of my 50th book. I'm both stunned and thrilled. I started my writing career dreaming of writing a Silhouette Desire MAN OF THE MONTH. Along the way, I've written series romance, single titles, anthologies and an online novel. I love that my true love, Silhouette Desire, yes, even a MAN OF THE MONTH, marks my 50th story. Hero Damien Medici is worthy to be a Man of the Month, if not Man of the Year. He's wounded, yet strong, wealthy and protective. All he needs is the right woman....

Watch for the stories of Damien's brothers coming in January 2010. The Medici men will steal your heart....

All the best,

Leanne Banks

LEANNE
BANKS

BILLIONAIRE
EXTRAORDINAIRE

Silhouette Desire

Published by Silhouette Books

America's Publisher of Contemporary Romance

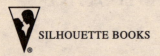 SILHOUETTE BOOKS

Recycling programs for this product may not exist in your area.

ISBN-13: 978-0-373-76939-1
ISBN-10:   0-373-76939-3

BILLIONAIRE EXTRAORDINAIRE

Books by Leanne Banks

Silhouette Desire

Royal Dad #1400
Tall, Dark & Royal #1412
His Majesty, M.D. #1435
The Playboy & Plain Jane #1483
Princess in His Bed #1515
Between Duty and Desire #1599
Shocking the Senator #1621
Billionaire's Proposition #1699
†*Bedded by the Billionaire* #1863
†*Billionaire's Marriage Bargain* #1886
Blackmailed Into a Fake Engagement #1916
†*Billionaire Extraordinaire* #1939

*The Royal Dumonts
†The Billionaires Club

LEANNE BANKS

is a *New York Times* and *USA TODAY* bestselling author who is surprised every time she realizes how many books she has written. Leanne loves chocolate, the beach and new adventures. To name a few, Leanne has ridden on an elephant, stood on an ostrich egg (no, it didn't break), gone parasailing and indoor skydiving. Leanne loves writing romance because she believes in the power and magic of love. She lives in Virginia with her family and her four-and-a-half-pound Pomeranian named Bijou. Visit her Web site at www.leannebanks.com.

This book is dedicated to all those who have helped me along the way, with special love to my mother, Betty Minyard. I am so blessed that you are my mother and my friend....

One

All she had to do was fake it.

All she had to do was act as if her insides matched the calm, competent, loyal, efficient and discreet surface she worked hard to maintain. Emma Weatherfield had been faking it since she was six years old. This should be no different.

At 6:45 a.m., the door to the corner office suite at Megalos-De Luca Enterprises opened and in walked a tall man with black hair and black eyes that seemed to sear her with appraisal.

Emma's stomach clenched. She hadn't expected him until later. She felt goose bumps rise to the surface of the skin on her arms as she stood to greet the man. She'd been told he looked like a handsome version of Satan and she couldn't disagree. She didn't see a millimeter of pity or softness in his hard face or hard body. The scar on his cheek only punctuated his ruthless reputation.

Her pulse raced, but she ignored her reaction. "Mr. Medici," she said.

"Emma Weatherfield," he said and extended his hand to hers.

She hesitated a beat before taking it. After all, he was here to take the company that had provided the only stability she'd experienced in her life and rip it to shreds. Despite protests from Megalos-De Luca's top management, the current chairman of the board, James Oldham, had insisted on hiring an outside firm to conduct a reorganization. Damien Medici had made his fortune eliminating jobs.

She had a job to do, she reminded herself, and slid her hand inside his warm, strong palm. He squeezed her hand with just the right pressure and held her gaze as she noticed the texture of his skin. The calluses on his palm surprised her. He was president of his own company; there was no need for him to perform any sort of manual labor.

She would learn the answer to that question. She would learn the answers to all her questions and those of her previous bosses. It was her job to learn everything she could about Damien Medici and report back to the people of Megalos-De Luca, to whom she owed her new life.

"Call me Damien when it's just the two of us. Mr.

Medici can be reserved for other times. I was told you were efficient, but I didn't expect you to arrive at the office so early on a Monday," he said with a hint of admiration.

"Habit," she said, removing her hand from his. "Since this was a new position, I wanted to be prepared."

"And are you?" he asked, glancing around the office suite.

No, she thought, and wished she weren't so viscerally aware of his power. "I'll let you be the judge of that."

He nodded and pushed open the door to the corner executive office that gave a sweeping view of the craggy, snowcapped mountains outside of Las Vegas. "Come in," he said. "I understand you've been with the company for six years."

"Yes, I have," Emma said. She followed him inside the large inner office, watching as he wandered around the room, checking out the equipment and the desk and giving a cursory glance to the view.

"According to your résumé, you climbed the ranks quickly, working for Alex Megalos for the last two years. MD," he said, shortening the company name by using the initials of the founders, "has been good to you. They've paid your tuition and given you flexible hours to complete your degree."

"All true," she said.

"I'm sure you're grateful," he continued, unbuttoning his jacket. "Perhaps so grateful that you don't want to see MD make any significant changes."

"I want MD to thrive. The current economy is difficult. I want only the best for MD's future," Emma said, giving her planned response. She sounded stilted to her own ears.

He studied her. She felt a shiver race through her, but refused to let it show.

"Even if it's necessary for MD to cut jobs?" he asked. "Even if I need to turn the regular way of business on its ear?"

"You're legendary in your field. I'm certain you will be looking out for the company's best interests. After all, that's what you're paid to do as an unbiased, professional contractor."

He paused a moment and a ghost of a smile crossed his face again. "Good," he said, as if he knew she was giving a performance. "In that case, I'd like to start with financial reports from all the company divisions."

She blinked. "I thought you might want to meet with some of the vice presidents first."

He shook his head and pulled a laptop computer from his bag, ignoring the first-class computer on his desk. "The VPs will try to clutter my analysis with emotion. I'll take the reports."

"Yes, sir. If you prefer a different desktop…" she began.

"I always use my own computer. I prefer the ease of taking it with me."

"We have memory sticks available for that if—"

He shook his head. "No problem. Give it to someone else and it will be one less expense for your company."

She nodded slowly. True, but it also meant she would have difficulty gaining access to his electronic files when the time came. She'd known this assignment was going to be difficult, but she hadn't realized just how difficult.

"Yes, sir," she said again, determined to learn something about him. "How do you take your coffee?"

"I prefer to have a coffeepot in my office. I pour my own."

Now that surprised her. He must have read her reaction on her face.

He gave a short laugh. "I'm not like your previous bosses. I wasn't raised in a home filled with servants. I can take care of myself."

She nodded, wondering if she'd heard just a drop of resentment in his voice about the affluent upbringing of Max De Luca and Alex Megalos. "Is there anything else I can get for you?"

He shook his head. "Thank you. Just the reports."

Poring over the initial reports, crunching numbers, Damien felt the quiet vibration of his Black-Berry and debated picking up. A call would break his focus and he despised that. Glancing at the caller ID, he recognized his brother Rafe's number and answered.

"What's up, Rafe?" he asked, stretching as he

glanced outside the window and saw the sun begin to set.

"I'm chilling on a yacht in Key West. When are you going to pry yourself away from your job and come down and let me beat you at pool?"

Damien rose from his desk. "You're as much a workaholic with your yacht business as I am in my field."

"You must be afraid I'm gonna beat you bad," Rafe said.

Damien chuckled. He and Rafe had traded wins and losses playing pool since the two had reconnected as adults. "I won last time."

"Rematch," Rafe said crisply.

"Not anytime soon. My current contract will demand all my attention. James Oldham, Megalos-De Luca's new chairman of the board, has contacted me to reorganize Megalos-De Luca Enterprises."

Silence followed. "You always said you would find a way to pay back the De Lucas for what they did to our grandfather. I wondered how you'd pull that off."

"Funny how hard you have to work for some things, while others practically fall into your hands," Damien said. He'd dreamed of this day, this opportunity to bring down the De Luca name. The impact of the De Lucas' destruction of the Medici heritage had repercussions in future generations. Damien had always felt it was his job to make the De Luca family feel the same pain.

"Have you started yet?"

"Today," Damien said, feeling a surge of adrenaline at the realization. "I've been given an office at the Megalos-De Luca headquarters for my convenience."

Rafe laughed. "Talk about letting the fox in the henhouse."

"You could say that. I've also been supplied with a pretty little assistant," Damien said. "She's as loyal as the day is long."

"You have plans to change that," Rafe ventured.

"I'll do whatever is necessary," Damien said, intrigued by the thought of finding out what was underneath Miss Weatherfield's proper exterior. With forget-me-not-blue eyes, silky brown hair and a body he suspected held dangerous curves, she made him wonder what she was like in bed. Finding out could be a secondary bonus.

"Be careful," Rafe said.

Damien frowned at the odd remark. "Of what?"

"You've made your reputation and fortune by your ability to make unemotional decisions. You've got a lifetime of revenge riding on this contract. That's a helluva lot of emotion."

Damien considered his brother's advice, then firmed his resolve. "No need to worry about me, little brother. I've always led with my mind. This time will be no different."

"Okay. I've got your back if you need me," Rafe said. "Except when we're shooting pool."

Damien cracked a slight grin. "Thanks. Maybe I'll

take you up on your offer after I'm done here. We'll have something to toast. Take care," he said, and turned off his phone.

By the following afternoon, Damien had slashed seventy-five positions on the organizational chart. He planned to pull two of his best employees off their current assignments so they could perform individual analyses on each work group. The board had offered to give him MD employees to do the reviews, but Damien knew objectivity was key.

At four o'clock, a knock on his door interrupted his evaluation. "Yes," he said.

Emma peeked through the door and shook a paper bag. "I'm sorry to bother you, but I noticed you hadn't eaten, so…"

Her thoughtful gesture took him by surprise. He'd been clear that he would take care of himself. He waved his hand. "Come on in. What do you have?"

"I didn't know what you liked," she said, walking through the door.

He noticed she wore a conservatively cut black jacket and skirt that hinted at curves underneath. No sign of cleavage, and the skirt hit just below her knee, exposing shapely calves. He couldn't help wondering how she would look in something more revealing. "Then how did you choose?"

She opened her pink mouth and stared at him for a beat as if he'd caught her off guard. "I guessed. Roast beef on rye with brown mustard, lettuce and tomato."

His lips twitched. "Red meat," he said. "You didn't think I was a vegetarian."

She bit her lip and smiled tentatively. "Wild guess. I passed up the quiche, too."

He chuckled, reaching for the bag. "Thank you. You did a good job. Plain chips," he noted.

"I played it safe," she said in a neutral tone.

"So you did. If you've always been so adept at reading your employers' appetites, I can see why you were promoted."

Her eyes widened. "It was just food. It isn't that difficult. Alex liked anything with olives. Max skipped pasta and carbs at lunch because he always wanted to be sharp for the afternoon."

"And what about you?"

"Whatever I pack," she said. "May I get anything else for you?"

"Whatever you pack," he repeated, ignoring her question. "There's a company cafeteria."

"Habit," she said with a shrug that drew his gaze to her slim shoulders. "I've been packing my lunch since elementary school."

"Same here," he said. "When there was food available."

She gave him a silent, questioning glance.

"Foster homes," he said.

"Oh," she said, a combination of sympathy and confusion flitting through her eyes. "My father died when I was young, so it was just my mother and me."

He met her gaze and felt a lightning-fast connection that took him by surprise. He saw the same surprise cross her face as she blinked and looked away.

"I hope you like the—"

"Emma," a male voice called from the outer office. "Emma, are you there?"

Damien watched her cringe. "Just a second," she whispered and walked to the doorway. "Brad, I'm assisting Mr. Medici—"

"You can go ahead and—" Damien broke off, surprised when she desperately waved her hand behind her back for him to stop speaking.

Surprise lashed through him at her silent order. Or, was it a plea?

"No, tonight's not good. I need to work on a paper for one of my classes. Please excuse me," she said and turned back to Damien, closing the door behind her.

She met his gaze for a moment, then bit her lip. "Sorry about that. I'll just—"

Curious despite himself, Damien lifted his hand. "Who's Brad?"

She gave a heavy sigh. "He's a very nice man in accounting. Very kind. I can't think of a bad thing to say about him."

He nodded silently. "Except he doesn't take a hint well."

She closed her eyes and nodded. "He's very nice—"

"You've said that twice," he said.

"I don't like hurting people's feelings," she admitted. "Especially nice people."

"He's not all that nice if he's ignoring your rejections," he said. "I've learned that most nice people prefer honesty even when it hurts."

"I haven't been dishonest," she said.

"I'm sure you haven't."

Silence hung between them as she gnawed her lip. "He's asked me out at least a dozen times."

"And you've said no each time?" Damien said, incredulous. "The guy's head must be made of concrete."

She winced. "I might have visited his mother in the hospital once."

A soft heart beneath that crisp suit, he decided, and found the quality appealing. He shrugged. "You want me to see if he's on my list for terminations?"

Emma gasped. "Oh my goodness, no. I couldn't live with myself if I ever—" She shook her head. "No. He's an excellent employee. Honestly."

He regarded her silently for another long moment. She blinked and cleared her throat as if she were gathering her composure. "Well, I, uh, should let you eat your sandwich. If you need anything…"

"You'll know," he said.

Emma closed the door to Damien's office behind her and wanted to melt into the hardwood floor. Mortified, she covered her face with her hands. What was wrong with her? She prided herself on her ability to present a calm demeanor in every situation. Yet she'd been *babbling* to Damien Medici.

She'd worked for Max De Luca, who'd been called

the man of steel. She may have felt intimidated at times, but she'd managed to hold her own. For Alex Megalos, she'd maintained the highest level of discretion. Given his playboy reputation before he married Mallory James, she'd encountered more than a few phone calls from overzealous wannabe girlfriends.

Yet here, she'd glimpsed slices of humanity, even humor, when she'd expected Damien to be a block of ice. She found his strength and complexity compelling, almost seductive.

Appalled at the notion, she castigated herself. "Ridiculous," she muttered. Damien Medici was going to slice MD to shreds. He was the enemy.

Two

The next morning, Emma walked into Max De Luca's office suite to give him an update on Damien Medici. She felt a combination of nerves and disappointment as she faced Max, a tough VP whose heart had softened because of his wife Lilli and his son David.

"The only thing I know is that he has already begun to put together a termination list and that he asked for information from these departments." She handed her former boss a typed report.

Max glanced over the report. "What about the computer?"

"He's using his own laptop and told me to give the desktop to someone else who needs it. He uses his cell phone for all his calls, except for people inside the company. I included those calls on the report."

"I see," he said, thoughtfully reviewing the information. "Based on this, I think he'll start cuts in middle management."

Emma bit her lip.

Max shrugged. "I agree that MD needs to streamline. I just want to make sure we don't cut anything vital to our future. Middle management isn't a bad place to start, as long as he doesn't want to cut too deeply," Max conceded. "Both Alex and I agree that Medici isn't the right man for this job, but James Oldham is determined to stay on the side of the stockholders. He has won the position of chairman of the board, and he clearly intends to keep it. He is the most dictatorial chairman I've ever encountered at MD. Keep me posted. Let's meet next Tuesday at the same time."

"I'm sorry I don't have more information," she said.

Max gave a cynical smile. "Medici's no fool. He clearly trusts no one. If you learn anything new, use your cell to call my cell or Alex's."

"Of course," she said and left his office. She took the elevator down two floors to Damien's office suite.

As she entered the office, she was surprised to see a light shining from beneath the door to the inner office. The door was slightly ajar and she could hear Damien's voice. Stepping closer, she listened.

"Mr. Oldham, if you truly want Megalos-De Luca to be at the top of its game, you'll have to give me free rein on the cuts. I accepted this contract with you based on your promise to let me do what I do best. If you're finding our agreement difficult, I can leave today."

Emma dropped her jaw in shock. James Oldham was chairman of the board. *No one* dared speak to him in such a way.

"I've been through this many times, Mr. Oldham. I understand you're concerned about bad PR. A well-publicized termination package and a reemployment assistance program will go a long way to softening the blow." Damien paused for a second. "What's your answer? Will you give me the latitude you promised or not?"

Several seconds passed and Emma held her breath. If only James Oldham would just say *no,* then no one at the company would need to deal with him, including her.

"I thought you would see it my way," Damien said in a triumphant tone.

Emma's heart sank.

"I'll be in contact soon," Damien said, his voice louder as he moved closer to the door.

Emma fought a sliver of panic. He could *not* find her eavesdropping. She quickly moved to her desk and began to hum an off-key version of a song by Fergie as she turned on her desktop and set down her lunch and purse.

"Emma," Damien said from behind her.

Despite the fact that she knew he was there, she jumped. "Oh, hello. You're here very early."

"As are you," he said, studying her.

She prayed he couldn't read her mind. "I have this new boss who is even more of an early bird than I am. It's a real challenge to out-early him."

His lips twitched. "I don't expect you to work the kind of hours I do. I've been described as a workaholic by more than one person."

"And are you?" she asked, thankful for the diversion.

"I've never been afraid of hard work. That attitude has served me well. My work is my passion. My mistress."

"But don't you want human companion—" She quickly realized she'd stepped outside the line of professionalism and broke off. "I apologize. That's none of my business."

"You're correct. It's not, but I could ask you the same question."

Emma thought of her mother and all the money and effort it had required to get her out of trouble. Time and time again. "I have family."

"So do I. Brothers," he said. "We made contact again after we became adults."

The way he looked at her made her feel as if he could see inside her. There was a terrifying sexiness to his power. She suspected that he was the kind of man who could make a woman do anything he wanted and make her like it, too.

She wanted to withdraw from his appeal. She wanted not to feel the pull toward him, the forbidden attraction. She wanted to be able to be perfectly professional, perfectly removed. And she would.

"So you do," she said. "Forgive me. I've gotten off track. What can I get for you?"

For just three seconds, his gaze flicked over her with a heat that burned through her gray Ann Taylor suit, white blouse and maybe even through her department store bra and panties to the soft flesh beneath.

Emma held her breath.

"I'm still making evaluations based on the reports I've received. I'll be asking for information from other departments later today."

Emma's breath came out in a whoosh which she attempted to hide. She clasped her hands together. "Okay. Just let me know," she said and watched Damien return to his office and close the door.

"Get yourself together," she told herself. The only difference between Damien and her previous bosses was that Damien was worse, far worse. And far more forbidden.

The following day at lunch, Lilli De Luca burst through the door to Damien's outer office suite with her baby David in her arms. "Hi, Emma! We've missed you."

David, with his curly hair and bright blue eyes, beamed. "Mmm," he said as he looked at Emma.

Emma couldn't help smiling back at him. "What a sweetheart. Omigoodness, look at how he's grown," she said, extending her arms.

David went to her willingly. Emma dipped slightly under his weight and glanced at Lilli. "He's gained."

Lilli smiled and groaned at the same time. "Tell me something I don't know."

"He's so friendly, though. I thought he would be clingy," Emma said, bouncing as the baby stuffed his fist into his mouth. "Teething?"

Lilli nodded. "I'm told he's in that in-between stage. A few more months and he'll get clingy."

"He's gorgeous," Emma said. "And such a sweetie."

Lilli smiled with pride. "I couldn't agree more. Max is busy on a conference call. He told me a visit from David and me would cheer you up. How's it going?"

"It's going," Emma said because nothing else really seemed appropriate.

Damien's door swung open and he glanced at the three of them. He lifted his eyebrow in inquiry at Emma. "Mrs. De Luca," he said.

"And David," Emma added.

"Call me Lilli," Max's blond wife said. "How are you?"

"Fine, thank you. And you?"

Lilli smiled, glancing at David. "Busy. I see you won the lottery and got Emma assigned as your assistant."

He gave a slight nod. "Yes."

"Alex and Max have been locked in warfare over who gets Emma as their assistant. Consider yourself very lucky," she said.

"I do," he said, glancing at Emma and then at the baby. "This is Max's son?"

Lilli nodded. "The joy of our lives."

David looked at Damien curiously and Damien

extended his hand toward the baby. David grabbed the man's thumb and tugged.

Damien smiled. "Strong grip," he said. "He will have a strong will."

"Not too strong, I hope," Lilli murmured. "Would you like to hold him?"

Damien hesitated. Something inside Emma forced her to move before he could respond. She pushed the baby against his chest and he instinctively cradled David in his arms.

"Hello, there," he said.

David stared at him, transfixed, then blew a bubble.

Damien's lips curved slightly. "David is a good name for you. I can see you throwing a rock and felling Goliath."

"A modern-day Goliath," Lilli said. "Who would that be today?"

Damien met her gaze. "Interesting line of thought," he said and passed the baby to his mother. He nodded. "It's a pleasure to see you again."

"And you," Lilli said. "You have a difficult job. I don't envy you."

"I lead with my mind, not my emotions," Damien said. "I perform best that way." He glanced at Emma. "I need reports from some additional departments."

More terminations, she thought, but schooled her expression. "Let me get my notepad."

"I should go," Lilli said. "It's good seeing you again, Emma. Call me sometime. We could meet for lunch."

"Thanks," Emma said, feeling a tightness in her

stomach. "That sounds great. Thank you for stopping by." She picked up a pad and headed for Damien's office.

Moments later, after he'd listed the departments, she nodded and rose from the chair in front of the desk.

"You look pale," he said. "You hate what I'm doing."

"You see revenue," she said. "I see people's lives and families."

"Ultimately," he said, "revenue affects people's lives and families."

"I suppose," she said, feeling tired.

"Take the rest of the day off," he said.

She snapped her head up. "I couldn't."

"Yes, you could and you will. I take care of my own. I've been a manager long enough to know when one of my employees needs a break. And you need one now." He waved his hand. "Go shopping, take a nap, sit by the pool. Do whatever women do to relax."

She smiled. "I don't shop to relax. I'm not a big napper. And in case you didn't notice, I'm not chasing a tan."

"I noticed," he said, his eyes slightly hooded. "Find a way to take a break. You need it." He glanced down at his laptop screen as if he were dismissing her.

She rose slowly, unable to look away from him. He was right, but sometimes she didn't know *how* to relax. "What about you?" she couldn't help asking, even though she should. "How do you relax?"

He lifted his head, meeting her gaze. Had she really dared to ask him that?

"I don't," he said. "It's not necessary for me."

She tried to bite her tongue, but her reply escaped despite her better judgment. "Pot. Kettle."

His eyes narrowed. "Go home."

"I will," she said. "But pot. Kettle. G'night."

Emma arrived home and checked her voice mail, bracing herself as she heard her mother's voice. She sounded fine, but Emma could never be quite sure. She dialed her mother in Missouri. "Hi, Mom. How are you?"

"Good," her mother said. "I worked at the drug-store today. There was a big sale on ibuprofen, so everyone was stocking up. It kept me busy. You'll be happy to know I didn't do any gambling."

"I am," Emma said.

"But it sure is boring as hell," her mother retorted when Emma failed to rise to the bait.

Emma's stomach twisted. "Boring as hell" was a red flag. It was one of the first signs that her mother was falling off the gambling wagon.

"Would you like me to come see you?" Emma asked. "I could probably come this weekend."

Emma's mother laughed. "No. I'm not in any trouble. You can stay where you are."

"Are you sure?" Emma asked. "Because I can—"

"No, no. You don't need to interrupt your schedule for me. We'll see each other in June. That will be just fine for me. Have you been out with any new men lately?"

"Work has been busy for me, too," Emma hedged. "I need to get used to my new boss." Emma wasn't sure that would be possible with Damien.

"Is he young and handsome? Maybe you could go out with him. I never understood why you didn't date your other bosses. They were young, handsome and rich."

Her mother just didn't understand. "Mom, part of the reason I've succeeded is because I keep my professional life separate from my personal life."

"What personal life?" her mother countered. "All you do is work or take classes. When are you going to do something fun?"

Emma bit her tongue. She hadn't had time for a lot of fun with her mother's gambling addiction. "When things settle down a little bit," she said and switched the subject. "Is everything okay with your apartment? You mentioned a problem with your garbage disposal."

Ten minutes later, she hung up and released a heavy sigh, but she couldn't escape her uneasiness. Emma's mother had left Las Vegas three years ago after Emma had bailed her out of another bad debt. The goal had been to remove her mom from temptation. So far, it had worked, but Emma never felt as if she could let down her guard.

With her salary, Emma could be living in a luxurious condominium if she chose. Instead she always felt as if she needed to save it all away just in case her mother faltered again.

At times her worry had consumed her—she'd only found relief in work or the classes she took. Lately, however, she'd found herself craving something more. Not gambling, thank goodness, but perhaps friendship or companionship. She'd shied away from close relationships partly because of her shame over her mother's problems, but it had been three years since her mother's last gambling incident. Maybe she should try going out. Emma pictured herself hitting the club scene and cringed. Doing laundry or charity work would be easier and more productive.

Despite the fact that she was aware of every move Damien made during the next week, Emma kept her professional facade firmly in place. Inside, she was insatiably curious. His scar fascinated her. She wondered how he'd gotten it. She wondered where he got those calluses on his hands and how they would feel touching her.

There was a ruthless, dangerous streak about him that intrigued her. He was clearly a predatory male— there must be a woman or *women* in his life. His sexuality was too strong for him to be a monk.

Exhausted by the time she arrived home at the end of the week, she went to bed early only to dream of him. In a steamy vision, he held her with his dark gaze, then took her into his arms. Her heart hammered against her chest and she knew she should pull back, but she couldn't find the energy or the will.

Suddenly his muscled chest was bare against hers,

his tanned skin gleaming in the moonlight. Her breasts grew heavy with arousal. Restlessness hummed in her blood. She arched against him, wanting more, wanting that firm mouth of his on hers. Standing on tiptoe, she opened her mouth as he dipped closer to her. Closer, closer… Anticipation vibrated through her. Almost…

The image turned black.

He disappeared.

Like magic, one second he was there, the next gone. Frustration coursed through her. Where had he gone? Why—

She made a muffled sound of dissatisfaction and was suddenly aware of her rapid breaths and the sheet twisted at her waist. Her eyelids fluttered and she opened her eyes to the semidarkness of her room and the whir of the ceiling fan overhead. Her body was hot, aroused, ready.

Emma covered her head with her hand and groaned. "Oh, no." It was bad enough that she couldn't stop being aware of Damien every second she was in the office. Now he was invading her dreams. She was going to have to do something drastic. She was going to have to take Mallory Megalos up on her offer to set Emma up on a blind date. Emma needed a distraction. A male one.

Three

A rare rainstorm hit the Las Vegas area as Damien left the MD parking lot in his Ferrari. The car was one of his indulgences and the only times he didn't drive it were during a hailstorm or in snow. About a mile from the office, he braked at a stoplight and caught sight of a stranded motorist on the side of the road.

Taking a second look, he realized the person wearing the bright yellow rain slicker looking beneath the hood of the subcompact was his assistant, Emma. Checking his rearview mirrors, he motioned for the driver in the next lane to let him pass. Moments later, he pulled into the parking lot and lowered his window.

"Need some help?" he asked.

Emma whipped her head around to gape at him. "Damien?"

"Yes. Do you need some help?" he repeated.

Her eyes wide with surprise, she shook her head. "No, I can handle it. I was just seeing if it was something obvious like a loose battery cable or something."

"And?" he prompted.

"And it looks like I'm going to have to call the car service. They guarantee to arrive in an hour, so I'll just wait in the car. Thanks, though."

"How were you planning to get home?" he asked.

She paused, then smiled. "Didn't think of that."

"I'll call my service and you can ride with me. Slide in," he said, unlocking the passenger door and pushing it open.

Emma hesitated, looking at the door with what appeared to be trepidation in her eyes. He wondered what could be going through her brain.

"Come on," he said. "You're just getting wetter."

"Okay," she said and he called his car service as she slammed her hood shut. He hung up just as she scooted into the leather seat. "Yikes, now I'm getting your seat wet."

"It'll dry," he said with a shrug and noticed her gaze lingering on his shoulders. She quickly glanced away, but he couldn't prevent a quick surge of pleasure at her admiration, although he suspected it was reluctant. She'd seemed remote to the point of skittishness this week. He'd thought it was due to her antipathy at his role in cutting jobs at MD. Now he wasn't so sure.

Her cell phone rang, interrupting the silence. She grabbed it from her bag and winced. "Oh, no." She pressed the call button. "I'm so sorry," she said. "I got stranded with car problems. May I reschedule?" She paused. "As late as possible," she said. "Next Wednesday at six-thirty, thank you so much."

"You sure I can't get you there tonight?" he asked.

She shook her head. "No. It's a gift certificate for a birthday present I never used. Hair, makeup, a makeover kind of thing. I decided I should finally take the plunge."

"Why? You look beautiful," he said.

Her cheeks flared with color. "Thank you. I just thought it was time for a change. You and I talked about how we don't have much of a social life, so I decided maybe I should try to get one. A social life," she clarified. "But don't worry. I won't let it interfere with my job."

"I'm sure it won't," he said. "Is Brad finally going to get a break?"

Emma shook her head. "No, but Mallory Megalos has been trying to set me up for ages. I may regret it. We'll see," she muttered and looked out the window. "Oh, look. The car service is already here."

"Do you have a garage you regularly use?" he asked, pushing open the driver's-side door.

"You don't have to go out there. You'll just get wet," she protested.

"I've been in worse situations. Give me your keys

and stay where you are. I'll handle this. What is the name of your garage?"

She oozed reluctance, but he felt a spurt of victory when he saw her cave. "Ray's Auto Service."

Emma sat in the car, stewing over her predicament. If her goal was to stay as far away from Damien as possible and to squelch her hyperawareness of him, she'd just lost what little progress she'd made over the last week.

Everything about him felt sexy and forbidden to her, and sitting so close to him in the car just made it worse.

He ducked inside the car and slid his fingers through his damp, dark hair. Droplets of water clung to his high cheekbones. She knitted her fingers together to keep from reaching to wipe the water from his tanned cheeks. Mere inches from him, she couldn't help staring at the sensual shape of his mouth.

She took a deep breath to clear her head and instead inhaled the combination of leather, rain and just a hint of his cologne.

He turned to meet her gaze. "It's all taken care of. You should get a call from the garage tomorrow morning."

"Thank you," she said, taking another deep breath in an effort to curb her frustration.

"Have you had dinner?" he asked.

"No, but—"

"I haven't either. Would you like to grab a bite?"

She bit her lip. "That's not necessary. You've already done enough."

"We may as well eat," he said. "Unless you had other plans."

"No," she said reluctantly.

"Okay. Do you like seafood?"

"Love it," she confessed.

His mouth turned upward into a sexy smile that made her stomach dip. "Good. I do, too."

He drove to one of the most exclusive restaurants in Vegas and pulled his car to the valet at the entrance. Three young men stepped toward the car, appearing to salivate at the chance to drive the vehicle. One opened the door for her. "Welcome, miss," he said.

Rising from the car, Damien nodded toward the young man who had greeted Emma. "You," he said and tucked a large bill in the man's hand along with his key. "The name is Medici. Treat her nicely," he said.

The young man smiled and handed Damien a valet parking ticket. "Like a baby."

Damien stepped beside Emma and escorted her through the door. "How did you decide which one should take your car?"

"Easy," he said. "The one with the best manners. He helped you out of the car."

The maître d' took her coat and handed it off to an assistant hostess.

"Hmm," she said, impressed. "I feel a little under-dressed," she said. "When you said a bite to eat, I didn't expect this."

"You don't like it?" he asked.

"I didn't say that," she said, glancing around at the chic, sophisticated décor and the chic, sophisticated clientele. "I've never been here."

"And you live in Vegas?" he said in surprise. "Even I knew about this place and I'm new to town."

She shook her head, but couldn't help smiling. "You forget. I pack my lunch."

"Ah, well, not tonight," he said. Seconds later, they were guided to a table for two next to a window with a view of a fountain.

"This is lovely," she said. "I feel guilty."

"Don't. It will be nice for me to look at something besides reports while I eat dinner at my desk."

"I don't think you would have a difficult time finding someone to fill this chair," she said.

"But they wouldn't fill it like you do," he said, then glanced at the wine list. "White or red?"

"Either," she said, still hanging on his comment about how she filled the chair. What did he mean by that? "Whatever you prefer."

"What do *you* prefer?" he asked, meeting her gaze across the candlelit table.

"White," she said.

"Good," he said, and the candlelight glinted off his scar. Although she didn't want to stare, the jagged line captured her attention and curiosity. She caught his quick glance and tried to look away.

The waiter arrived and she forced herself to look at the menu. After they placed their orders and the waiter returned with their wine, Damien lifted his glass to her. "To a rare rainstorm, car trouble and a mutual appreciation for seafood."

She smiled and nodded, lifting her glass to clink against his. "Here, here," she said softly and swallowed a sip of the fragrant Pinot Grigio. "Very good."

"Yes," he said as she took another sip. "I noticed you staring at my scar."

The wine caught in her throat and she coughed. She cleared her throat several times, wishing he hadn't seen her looking at him so intently. "I'm sorry," she finally managed. "That was rude."

"No, it wasn't," he said. "Natural curiosity."

She couldn't think of a good response, so she said nothing and didn't attempt to push any more wine through her tight throat.

"You wonder how it happened, don't you?"

She sucked in a quick breath. "It's none of my business."

One side of his mouth lifted in a cryptic smile. "But you still want to know. How do you think I got the scar?"

She blinked at his question. How in the world should she know? But she had imagined. She'd visualized several scenarios. Dare she share them?

"Your mind is turning a mile a minute," he said, far too accurately. "Go ahead, tell me how you thought I got the scar."

Emma closed her eyes for a second, then for some wild, unreasonable reason, she decided to play along.

"You were in a bar fight and a drunk went after you with a broken bottle."

He cocked his head to one side and lifted his wineglass for a sip. "Who won the fight?"

"You, of course," she said. "Or, you were a pirate on a ship and someone cut you with a sword."

He chuckled. "I like that one. How did I get off the ship?"

She shrugged. "You swung on some ropes and swam ashore. I loved Johnny Depp in his pirate movies."

He nodded. "Any other scenarios?"

"You faced a shady guy in an alley outside a nightclub. He went after you with a switchblade because you'd stolen his girlfriend."

"Interesting," he said. "How come I wasn't the shady guy?"

"Well, in a way you were because you stole his girlfriend," she said.

He lifted a dark eyebrow. "You think I'm shady?"

She winced, realizing she'd gone too far. "This was all supposition. Crazy scenarios."

He nodded and took another sip. "Your first scenario was closest. I got into a fight with one of my foster fathers. He was beating my foster mother. I was thirteen. I had my fists. He had a beer bottle. My foster mother stayed. I was reassigned."

"Oh," she said, feeling the weight of that moment on her chest. "That's horrible."

He shrugged. "I survived my childhood. Not everyone does."

Emma couldn't help wondering what other scars he carried as a result of his upbringing. His effort to protect his foster mother had been heroic, but it hadn't been rewarded.

"Now I've frightened you," he said.

"No," she said quickly, shaking her head. "The thought of you going through that as a young man," she said, taking a quick breath. "It hurts."

"You have a tender heart. Your mother must have loved you well."

"She did the best she could," Emma said.

He wrinkled his brow slightly as he studied her and she felt compelled to explain. "You know how some people have a drinking problem?" she asked and he nodded. "She had…has a gambling problem."

He gave a slow nod. "That must have been tough."

"It was. Sometimes, it still is. But she doesn't live in Vegas anymore, so that's a good start." Emma felt uncomfortable beneath his scrutiny. "Enough of that. Where did you live before you came here? How are you dealing with our lack of humidity?"

"I had a long-term assignment in Minnesota, so I find this a nice change. I build houses for charity," he said.

"Really?" she said. "I'd wondered where you got those calluses on your hands."

"You noticed," he said, his dark eyes glinting with sensuality again.

Her breath stopped somewhere in her chest. "Yes, I guess I did," she reluctantly admitted.

"With my job, I strip away the excess. To balance that, I help build up. The combination keeps me balanced."

She was caught off guard that he would feel the need to build anything. Ruthlessness seemed to come so easily to him.

"Your face is so easy to read. You look surprised."

Irritated that he seemed to have the ability to read her thoughts, she frowned, blurting out her thoughts. "Yes, I'm surprised. I thought you were a descendant of one of those pirates we were discussing a moment ago. I wouldn't have thought someone who cuts the livelihood of dozens of people without batting an eye would be interested in any kind of charity." She was horrified that he provoked her so easily. "I can't believe I just said that to my boss."

Damien gave a low chuckle. "I was told you're discreet and respectful. Is this how you talked with your previous bosses?"

"No," she said, shaking her head. "I'm extremely discreet. Ask Alex Megalos or Max De Luca. And I've always been respectful. It's you," she said. "You bring it out in me. This is crazy. I shouldn't be here. Perhaps I shouldn't be your assistant." She rose to her feet because she couldn't stand embarrassing herself further.

"Sit down," he said. "Our dinner is on the way.

There's no need to waste a good meal just because you think I'm the kind of man to eat small children for breakfast."

When she didn't immediately comply, he lifted an eyebrow.

Sighing, she sank into her chair. "I wouldn't have said small children."

"Okay," he said. "Pretty assistants who tell the truth."

He'd just called her pretty. She felt a rush of pleasure. Heaven help her, this was crazy. She felt like a double agent. She'd prejudged Damien and he was scrambling her preconceptions of him. He was scrambling her hormones, too. She couldn't help wondering what it would be like to kiss him, and more.

The waiter served plates with presentations of gourmet fish and vegetables.

"Tell me more about you," he said. "You've made me curious."

She felt a clench and swallowed. "No need to be curious. I'm boring. Really boring."

"Favorite music," he countered.

She shrugged. "Maroon 5. Fergie. Michael Bublé. Van Morrison. Delbert McClinton."

"Van Morrison and Delbert McClinton," he echoed. "They don't fit."

"They're wonderful. They don't need to fit," she said, unable to squelch a smile.

He slowly lifted his lips in a return smile. "I like that."

He said it as if he found her interesting, perhaps

even alluring. The notion was as heady as three glasses of champagne, but Emma was determined not to sink further under his spell. Focus on the meal, she told herself. Not the man.

Two hours later, with the rainstorm at an end, Damien drove her home to her safe, modest apartment complex on the outskirts of town.

"Maintenance should repair that light," Damien said as he pulled to a stop just outside her apartment.

"I'll remind them tomorrow. Thank you for everything," she said. "Rescuing me in the rain, dinner. Thank you."

He cut the engine. "No problem. I'll walk you to your door."

Surprised, she shook her head. "Oh, that's not necessary. My door is in sight."

"I wouldn't be a gentleman if I didn't walk you to your door," he said.

"I thought we had established that you are a pirate, not a gentleman," she whispered.

He chuckled. "I'll walk you to your door," he said and got out of the car.

Emma sighed, wishing he weren't so attractive, wishing she weren't fascinated by him. He opened her passenger door and helped her out. His hand was strong, his body emanated a heat that tempted her to lean into him. She resisted the urge.

Feeling the light touch of his hand against the small of her back, she walked toward her door.

Rattled by his effect on her, she rummaged inside her purse for her key, finally locating it. She jammed it into the lock and turned. It took a few tries, but the lock finally released and her breath did the same.

She opened the door and turned to him. He was far too close. "Thank you again," she murmured, hyperaware of his tall, muscular form. "For everything."

"My pleasure," he said.

Eager to escape his effect on her, she scrambled forward, falling. She was certain she would land flat on her face, but Damien caught her. His strong arms wrapped around her, drawing her back against his muscular body. Her breath stopped in her chest.

Whoa, girl. Get yourself under control. She put her hand on one of his forearms to remove it, but was immediately distracted by the way his muscles rippled beneath her touch.

"Are you okay?" he asked, his mouth inches from her ear. The sound was low and intimate, filling her with instant heat.

Emma swallowed over her dry throat and nodded. "Yes, I'm fine. I just lost my balance." She deliberately stepped away from him and turned around. "Thanks," she said. "Again. I'll see you tomorrow."

"Not unless you have another ride," he corrected. "I can pick you up. Is seven-thirty okay?"

Emma blinked, remembering that her car was in the shop. "Oh, that's not necessary. I can—"

"Do you have another ride?" he cut in.

"Not at the moment, but—"

"Then there's no reason for you to reject my offer, is there?"

His gaze could melt steel, she thought, and heaven knew she wasn't steel. "I guess not. I'll see you in the morning. Good night," she said, closing the door and leaning against it, praying for sanity.

Four

The next morning, Damien barely pulled into the parking lot just outside Emma's apartment before she opened her door and strode toward him. As usual, she wore a suit, this time dark slacks and a jacket with a white blouse underneath. Her silky light brown hair was tugged away from her face in a ponytail, emphasizing her delicate features and the contrast of her rosy lips with her pale skin.

Although he suspected her pantsuit was designed to disguise her long legs and feminine curves, he could see the promise of her feminine form beneath the business attire…creamy pale shoulders and breasts with rosy tips just a shade darker than her lips, a slender waist, round inviting hips and long, lithe legs that would wrap around a man's waist while he…

Putting his car in park, he got out and opened the car door just as she reached the car. "Good morning."

"Good morning," she said, her gaze skimming over him in appreciation before she glanced away and slid into the car. "Thank you."

Returning to the driver's seat, he felt her assess him again before she turned her head. It was as if she had a hard time resisting the urge to look at him. The knowledge shot through him with a secret pleasure.

Emma Weatherfield intrigued him more with each passing day. He'd already intended to get information from her regarding Max De Luca and Alex Megalos. Now that he knew she was attracted to him, he'd decided to satisfy his curiosity and hers in bed. MD had no rules against fraternization among employees, so there was no reason the two of them couldn't indulge.

"Did you sleep well?" he asked, putting the car into gear and driving out of the parking lot.

She slid a quick sideways glance at him, but kept her head facing forward. "Well enough. I don't require a lot of sleep."

"Neither do I. That helps when you're a workaholic."

Her lips turned upward slightly. "I guess it would. Did you work more last night?"

"For a while," he said. "Several things need to be in place when a company is making employee cuts, such as employment counseling, instructions for how to apply for unemployment, recommended programs for additional training and relocation information. Despite your belief that I'm a ruthless pirate with no consideration for human beings, I know there's a right way and a wrong way to make cuts. The people giving the notices will also need to be properly trained."

She gave a slow, reluctant nod. "If the cuts are absolutely necessary, then the employees need as many resources at their disposal as possible." She grimaced. "I wouldn't want to be the one delivering the news."

"With your soft heart, it would be difficult. But there are ways that make it easier for the person being released."

"I can't imagine what," she said.

"A matter-of-fact approach that offers the laid-off employee a measure of dignity is vital. There are even days of the week to try to avoid."

"Terminations on Friday?" she asked. "To give people a chance to recover from the blow."

"No, Friday is the worst day. The terminated employee is left to stew all weekend without an opportunity to receive support."

"You almost make it sound humane," she said, meeting his gaze with her blue eyes.

"I'm not out to destroy everyone's lives," he said, and thought of Max De Luca. He was just determined to settle a score with the family who had destroyed his.

Thirty minutes later, after he and Emma had

arrived at the office, Damien was clarifying some figures with one of his assistants who worked from home when he heard a loud voice in the outer office.

"He's a hatchet man. He's going to destroy our lives. All I want is one minute with him," a man said.

Damien immediately rose from his desk and rushed to open the door. Emma stood with her back to him.

"Mr. Harding, Mr. Medici is busy right now. He cannot take visitors without an appoint—"

"Let me at him," the heavyset man said, his face gleaming with perspiration.

"I'm Mr. Medici," Damien said, stepping in front of Emma, motioning her aside.

The man immediately turned his attention to Damien. "You," he said, pointing his finger at Damien. "You're going to ruin us."

"I have no intention of ruining you. Excuse me, we haven't met. My name is Damien Medici. And you are?"

The man blinked as if he were surprised at Damien's politeness. "I'm, uh—I'm Fred Harding and I heard my name is on your termination list. How am I supposed to feed my family if you fire me?" he demanded, rubbing his damp brow with his hand.

"The termination list hasn't been finalized. However, if your employment is terminated, then you will be given at least two weeks pay with employment and training counseling, plus you'll receive assistance on how to apply for unemployment benefits provided by the government."

Fred Harding met Damien's gaze, then glanced away and took a deep breath. "It's still tough."

Damien nodded. "It is, but I have to tell you that plenty of people turn this situation into a good change. I don't know if your position is on the line, but you can be one of those people who make this kind of change a positive one for yourself."

"We'll see," Fred said, wearing a look of resignation.

"Good luck," Damien said, extending his hand.

Fred accepted the handshake. "Thanks. I'll take it."

After the man walked out of the office, Emma audibly exhaled. Damien glanced at her.

"I thought I was going to have to call security," she said.

"So did I," Damien said. "This is crazy. I'm speaking to a board member today. The VPs have wanted to keep the reorganization quiet, but the uncertainty is just making everyone nervous. Productivity will go into the toilet. This kind of thing can't be kept secret. An assistant, cafeteria worker or janitor could find out and start spreading false rumours."

"What are you saying?"

"I'm saying I want an announcement to go out to all MD employees that a reorganization is taking place and what the minimum severance package will be. The first cuts should be taken no less than three weeks after that."

Emma's eyes widened. "Isn't that fast?"

"According to Fred, apparently not fast enough," Damien said. "I'm also going to get security on this floor. I'm not going to have you providing guard duty. If you get even a hint of a threatening attitude in a call or e-mail, then I want you to let me know immediately. In the meantime, the open door policy is over. From now on, lock the door and you and I both will use a key. Do you understand?"

Emma bit her lip. "Yes."

Damien returned to his office and Emma sank into her chair. She hated to admit it, but she had begun to feel a bit frightened by Fred Harding's desperation before Damien had intervened. From her experience with her mother and her mother's lenders, she'd learned that desperate people used desperate measures to protect themselves. Or irrational ones.

She was amazed at how quickly Damien had diffused the man's blustering, threatening demeanor. He'd stepped right in front of her. What if Fred had been carrying a weapon? The possibility made her break into a cold sweat.

His protectiveness did something to her, sent her into a whirl of confusion. She tried to remember when a man had been so blatantly protective of her, but she couldn't. Sure, Alex and Max had gone to bat for her professionally, but she couldn't recall when a man had come to her defense so readily.

Determined to collect herself, she poured a cup of coffee and booted up her computer, her mind speeding a mile a minute. The image of his strong back and the low but authoritative voice he used with Harding was stamped on her brain.

Damien was the kind of man who made other men back down simply by virtue of being. He oozed confidence and clarity.

She took a sip of her coffee as he returned to the outer office. "Have you locked the door?"

She shook her head. "No, I—" She didn't want to show how much the incident had affected her. "I'll do it right away."

She rose and he snagged her wrist. "Are you okay?"

"It just took me off guard," she said. "It's not something that happens every day." She forced a little laugh. "Well, there was that one woman who stalked Alex for a while…" When he lifted his eyebrow, she rushed to correct herself. "Just kidding."

He looked into her eyes with deadly intent on his face. "I won't let anyone hurt you," he said.

A tremor shook her all the way to her toes. She knew with certainty that he could and would protect her. It tripped off wishes she'd kept locked away for years—the fantasy that a man would stick with her through the rough times.

He was talking about work, she reminded herself. It wasn't personal, but his hand wrapped around her wrist certainly felt that way. Maybe she secretly wanted it to be personal.

Appalled at the direction of her thoughts, she pulled her hand from his. "Hopefully, it won't be an issue."

He nodded. "It won't be," he said in a crisp voice. "If you're recovered—"

"I am," she quickly said, stiffening her spine against his effect on her.

"Then I'd like you to draft a letter for all of the employees informing them of the reorganization plans. After it's finalized, I'll discuss it with a board member and we should send it out no later than tomorrow."

Taken off guard yet again, she forced a nod. "Okay. I'll just need the details."

"I've already e-mailed them to you," he said. He walked to the outer office suite door and turned the lock.

The room immediately seemed to shrink, and as he walked closer to her, the oxygen seemed to disappear. Was she trapped in here with the devil or the man in her fantasies?

"I'll be on the phone for the next hour, but if you run into any problems, don't hesitate to interrupt."

Fighting the sense that she was aiding and abetting a slasher, Emma constructed the letter and revised it twice after suggestions from Damien. Her stomach remained in a knot the entire morning. She knew she had to inform Max or Alex about this latest development, but the earliest she could manage it would be during her lunch hour.

Scooting out of her office a few minutes early, she left a note for Damien and rushed to Max's office, but he wasn't there. She tried Alex, but he was also out of the office.

Fretting, she went outside for a walk and called Max's personal cell phone number as he'd asked. When the call went immediately to voice mail, her frustration spiked. Her lunch hour nearly over, she visited Max's office once more, only to find him still gone. She swung by Alex's with matching luck and, despairing, headed for the elevator.

The doors opened and Alex appeared, smiling when he saw her. "Emma, what a nice surprise to see you. Mallory's been after me to make sure you're attending that charity gala she's planning in a few weeks. She's determined to hook you up even though I told her that you're the most content single woman I know."

"Mallory's a sweetheart. I've got the charity gala on my calendar." Emma glanced at her watch. Her time was running out. "Do you have a minute?"

"Sure. What do you need?"

"In your office?"

Alex must have picked up on her nervousness because his expression sobered. "Of course," he said and led the way to his office. "Marlena, hold my calls for the next few minutes," he said to his assistant. As soon as Emma stepped inside his private office, he closed the door. "News?"

She nodded, feeling a knot form in her throat. Her sense of loyalty was torn. On the one hand, she owed Alex and Max her college education and her future. On the other hand, Damien was her boss and he believed he was doing the best thing for MD.

"He's going to the board. He's determined to send a letter to all employees informing them of the impending layoffs and the minimum compensation they can expect. I think he wants to make the first cuts within a few weeks."

Alex stared at her in shock. "I didn't think he would move this quickly."

"I've never seen anyone so focused. He has very specific ideas about how the layoffs should be announced and conducted, down to the day of the week."

"Which day?" he asked.

"Not Friday," she said. "He seems to prefer Tuesday or Wednesday to give people a chance to access support services."

"Unless we find a way to stop him, he's going to change the entire culture of the company," Alex said grimly. "How can MD continue to progress with all these cuts? Granted the stock dividends are down, but whose aren't? A panic cut is going to bite into our chances for future profits."

Emma couldn't disagree. "Unless you can find a way to get someone on the board to agree with you…" She felt duplicitous even saying such a thing. "I'm sorry I don't have better news."

"No," Alex said. "You did what you were supposed to do. Keep us posted."

Nodding, she left his office. She'd thought she could do this job without it bothering her, but now she felt ripped in half, dirty almost. Distracted as she walked down the hallway, she pushed the button for the elevator. Seconds later, the doors opened and she found herself face-to-face with Damien.

Damien felt the slightest twist in his gut at the expression on Emma's face. Guilt, he saw it in her clouded blue eyes, her eyebrows knitted with worry. Poor thing, she made a terrible double agent.

"Miss Weatherfield," he said, because he always addressed staff formally when in public. "What a surprise to meet you here on the executive floor."

"I—uh, I ran into Mr. Megalos and he wanted to discuss the invitation his wife had extended to me for a charity gala in a few weeks," she said.

He nodded. The truth was she'd run upstairs to tell Alex what Damien was planning to do. As if Alex or Max could change it. Damien knew they couldn't. "What charity gala is this?"

"Uh, I believe it's for cancer research. It's on a Saturday, the week after next."

"I've intended to participate in a charity drive since I've been in Vegas, but I've been busy. Perhaps you would allow me to escort you," he said.

Her jaw dropped and she moved her mouth, but no sound came out. She cleared her throat. "I—uh—"

"Unless you already have an escort," he said.

"No, but—"

"But?" he echoed.

"I may be helping Mallory, so I wouldn't be able to give you the attention you deserve," she said.

"I'm not high-maintenance," he said with a

slight smile. "I can look after myself once we arrive. Date?"

She bit her lip and looked at him with a frightened expression. "I guess so. I'll uh, head back to the office, Da—" She broke off. "Mr. Medici."

He gave a short nod and watched her step quickly into the elevator. The doors closed and he stood there for a moment. He wasn't surprised that Emma was reporting to her previous managers. Heaven knew, this had happened to him many times before.

Her guilt was actually a promising sign. It meant he had begun to chip away at her loyalty. It meant she felt conflicted, which meant she didn't see him as a total sonovabitch out to destroy MD.

It meant he could possibly win her over to his side. She had the information he needed to take down Max De Luca. Emma was highly intelligent and had a knack for reading people. Her calm attitude encouraged disclosure, and Damien was certain she knew secrets about both her bosses. Secrets he intended to learn. He would use any method to gain her assistance, including seduction. In fact, seducing Emma could very well be the best side benefit of taking this assignment.

Five

Emma spent the entire weekend cleaning and re-cleaning her apartment, but she still felt scummy. She suspected this was some sort of Lady Macbeth-esque response to her subterfuge at work. She had a hard time looking herself in the eye in the mirror, let alone meeting Damien's gaze on Monday morning.

With the doors locked, she was even more aware of him than usual. Was she imagining it or was his body brushing hers more often? Did he notice how his hand covered hers on the doorknob?

She found herself desperate to turn down her internal heat and maintain a business attitude toward him. Why did her mind persist in imagining him shirtless with his chest pressed against hers, his strong arms wrapped around her? Why did she find herself forcing her gaze from staring at his mouth, wondering how his lips would feel on hers?

None of this made sense. She'd been assistant to two very attractive and powerful men before. Why did Damien affect her this way? She felt as if she had suddenly gone man-crazy, except her lunacy was very specific.

Thank goodness, a distraction appeared. She grasped at it. The salon offering her a full makeover called to schedule an appointment since they'd had a cancellation for Monday. During her pedicure, Mallory called and set Emma up with a date on Tuesday night.

Emma didn't care if the guy was an axe murderer. She just needed someone to get her mind off her boss. Staring into the mirror at the end of her make-over, she was stunned at the transformation. With a few sunny streaks and her hair styled in a sexy shoulder-length cut, smoky eyes and plump lips, she actually looked hot. Gulp. Although she wasn't sure she could duplicate the job the experts had done on her, she would give it her best try since she was meeting her blind date for cocktails and dinner.

The following day, she walked into the office with an extra little bag that contained her cosmetics and change of clothes for her date. She heard Damien on the phone, but he finished before she had a chance to discern anything about his conversation.

He entered the outer office and nodded at her. "Good morning," he said as he reached to lock the door.

"Good—" She noticed the white bandage around his left hand. "Oh, no, what happened?"

He shrugged. "A minor accident last night. It was teen night for Rebuilding Vegas. The idea was to teach practical construction skills to local kids."

Emma grimaced. "Sounds like it was dangerous."

"Someone dropped a saw from the second floor. I tried to catch it so no one would get hurt."

"But you got hurt."

"A few stitches. I'll live."

"Bet they offered pain medication, and you wouldn't take it," she ventured.

His lips twitched. "It wasn't necessary."

"Of course it wasn't," she said. "You probably need to chew glass in order to be happy."

He gave a low chuckle. "You're in a snappy mood today. Any reason why?"

"Not really," she said, thankful that she had a date tonight. A date that would hopefully take her mind off Damien. Heaven help her, the man was burning up her dreams and fantasies. She could only hope that whoever she met tonight would be able to distract her.

He narrowed his eyes. "Your hair looks different," he said.

"Very observant," she said. "I got it cut last night."

"That's not all. There's something else."

"The hairstylist added a few highlights," she said, uncomfortable under his intent gaze.

"Nice," he said. "But it looked good before. Ah, this was your makeover. I thought you weren't going until Wednesday."

He'd remembered, she thought, and her discomfort grew. "They had an opening."

"They changed your hair. What else?"

She cleared her throat. "Just chose a couple new outfits for me to wear and some different makeup. The makeup is more appropriate for after work. I have some for to—" She broke off, not wanting to reveal any more. "I'm sure there are more important topics for us to discuss. Did you want me to gather any reports for you today?"

Feeling him watch her in silence, she fought the urge to fidget.

"Yes. As a matter of fact, I do. I want to do a closer study on the San Diego resorts."

"I'll get them for you," she said. "You had mentioned you hadn't wanted to talk to any of the VPs involved with the departments you're studying. Should I assume you prefer to take the same approach with this one?"

He shook his head. "No. As a matter of fact, I want to talk with Alex or Max, but I'll arrange that myself."

Frustration rippled through her. "As you wish. Is there anything else?"

"Not right now," he said.

Without realizing it, she released that sigh she'd been holding as she turned away.

"You're displeased," he said.

"I'm sorry. I didn't mean to come across that way," she said, sliding into her seat, damning herself for giving away her emotions. She really was supposed to be much better at conveying calm. She always had been before Damien had arrived.

"Any chance you can give me an honest answer to an honest question?" he asked, his bandaged hand resting on his lean hip.

"Of course I can," she said.

"Why did you sigh just a moment ago when I told you I have nothing else for you to do right now?"

Darn it. She should have held her breath. She reluctantly met his gaze. "If I'd known you were going to give me so little work to do, then I would have taken an extra online course this semester. You don't want me to make your coffee. You don't want me to set up appointments. I feel guilty spending so much time twiddling my thumbs."

His lips twitched. "A first," he said. "You're upset because I'm not giving you more work to do."

"Well, would you be happy?" she asked, her courage stemming from frustration.

He paused, looking at her in silence. "You have a good point. Okay, fine. I want you to take a look at the performance, expenses, employees—everything in connection with the San Diego resorts. And I want you to make a recommendation for job cuts."

She dropped her jaw. "Excuse me?"

"Yes. I'd like your recommendations within two days."

"Two days?"

"Do you have a problem with that? You've been trained to read a profit and loss statement. Despite the fact that you're an executive assistant, you've earned a degree in business. I think this assignment will help you gain some perspective."

She worked her mouth, then closed it and cleared her throat. "No. No problem. Thank you very much." She watched him walk into his office, the V-shape of his body distracting her. Until he closed his door.

Emma shook her head. *Crap.* This was what happened when she let down her guard. Damien now expected her to give him suggestions on his hatchet job. How was she supposed to do that?

Hours later, after skipping her lunch break, Emma felt as if her eyeballs were spinning. She had begun her assessment of the San Diego properties and tentatively put an X beside a few positions only to mark out her original X.

Just as she made the decision to cut a position, she began to think about the person in that position and how they would feel about having their job cut, what kind of family they supported. Several scenarios for each person came to mind, all of them making her feel like the Grinch.

Absently glancing at the clock, she was shocked by the late hour. She was supposed to meet Mallory's setup guy in thirty minutes. She had to stop working. Even though she'd essentially made zero progress, she had to stop. Hopefully a good night of sleep would provide her with a clear mind tomorrow so she could properly perform this assignment. In the meantime, she needed to remember how to make her eyes smoky, she thought as she grabbed her cosmetic bag and headed for the restroom.

Twenty minutes of swearing and perspiration later, she'd changed into her makeover outfit of a little black dress that showed a bit of cleavage and clung to her curves and returned to her desk to turn off her computer.

Hearing a sound in the outer office, Damien glanced away from his laptop, noting the tightness in his shoulders and neck. The sensations weren't unusual. He'd been known to go for hours completely focused on his task. He'd learned, however, that even he should take short breaks. He opened his door and glanced into the outer office, stopping short.

The sight of a woman wearing high heels and a body-skimming black dress that hugged her curves—in particular the backside currently facing him—took him off guard.

"Emma?"

She whirled around, her eyes wide and her plump lips parted in surprise. "Oops. I didn't hear you."

He stared at her face, taking in her sexy blue eyes and luscious mouth, pink and tempting. "Special occasion?"

She shrugged her shoulders, drawing his attention to her generous, creamy breasts. "One of Mallory's setups," she said with a lopsided smile. "We'll see."

"One," he echoed. "There's more than one?"

"That's up to me," she with a slight grimace as she grabbed her purse and a plastic bag. "She's very determined. She says crazy things like I'm an undiscovered treasure. Nice of her," she said, clearly embarrassed. "I should go. I'll see you in the morning."

He nodded. "Yeah. Have a good time."

"Hope so," she said with a smile and walked out of the office, her hips drawing his attention. He thought about putting his hands on her hips, taking her breasts into his hands and mouth, sliding between her thighs and feeling her femininity close around him like the most intimate, wet embrace.

Feeling himself grow hard, he was surprised at the force of his reaction to her. Plus, for some reason, he felt damn annoyed that she was seeing another man tonight. He was usually as detached about his sex life as he was about his professional life. He chose his partners for their ability to please him, and he'd never had a problem providing a woman with complete sexual satisfaction.

The truth was, however, that he tended to choose a more sophisticated woman than Emma, a woman who would respond to his needs and the passion of the moment and be satisfied with a brief affair, with perhaps an expensive trinket as a souvenir.

Despite her professional demeanor, he could

feel her curiosity about him growing stronger every day. She was drawn to him, he could see it in her eyes and hear it in her breath when he stepped close to her. He couldn't help wondering how hot he could make Emma, how she would feel in his arms, in his bed.

Damien gave a mental check of his calendar and a plan quickly formed in his mind. A surge of anticipation and satisfaction slid through him. Emma Weatherfield would be in his bed by the end of next week.

After a date where she could not stop comparing her setup guy to Damien, Emma felt like banging her head against the wall. Any wall, but especially her office wall because the next morning she found to her great disappointment that the setup date had provided her with zero distraction. A baby-faced blond sales rep for a paper company, Doug Caldwell had been full of smiles and eager to please. He reminded Emma of a puppy where Damien reminded her of a mysterious predator.

In addition, today she faced the ugly task of recommending which employees should be let go from their positions. By Thursday afternoon, she felt as if she may as well be playing Pin the Tail on the Donkey with the organizational chart. She hoped against hope that Damien was too busy and would forget to ask for her recommendations.

As if on cue, he opened the door to his office and shot her a look of inquiry. "Ready to give me your list?"

Dragging herself into his office with her final draft, she instinctively held the paper behind her back. "I feel I should warn you that I don't have your experience, so my recommendations may not be as helpful as you or I would like them to be."

He waved his hand. "Let me see them."

She reluctantly surrendered the paper to him and clenched her teeth as she waited for his response. He glanced at the paper, then at her. "Where are the rest of the recommended cuts?"

"Those are all," she said and cleared her throat.

"Two?" he said in astonishment. "You recommended two cuts?"

"Yes. Two," she said.

He rubbed his hand over his face and chuckled. "You do know that if you were ever promoted into management you would need to be able to fire an employee."

Her stomach knotted. "Yes."

"What was your major?"

"Business administration," she said.

He shook his head.

"But I think my natural skills are better in the areas of organizing and reducing expenditures through practical economic measures."

"Turn out the lights when you leave the room," he said.

"Yes. No new hires before you begin downsizing. No pay raises for executives. With the actual properties, initiating new incentive programs and perks for repeat customers. Since most of our properties are top-of-the-line luxury resorts, finding a way to lure new guests during the off-season would give new customers a taste of what it's like to stay at an MD resort. Once they've experienced it, they will want to repeat it."

He gave a slow nod. "Have you talked about these ideas with your former bosses?"

She shook her head. "I thought it would have been considered presumptuous."

"Do you want to advance at MD?"

"Of course I do," she said, unable to keep a trace of indignation from her voice.

"You underestimate yourself. I suggest you put together a report with your suggestions." He shrugged and sat down. "That's all."

She stared at him with an open mouth for several seconds before he raised his eyebrows at her. "Did you have a question?"

Blinking, she pulled herself together and backed away. "No." Returning to her desk, she fought a wave of confusion. Had Damien Medici just offered career guidance? Had he paid her a compliment? She felt a rush of pleasure. He certainly hadn't gushed, but he hadn't criticized her ideas, either.

Sinking into her seat, she was puzzled. If he thought she underestimated herself, why didn't he allow her to do more for him?

At the end of the day on Friday, Damien called her

into his office again. "What time should I pick you up tomorrow night?"

"Tomorrow night?" she echoed, confused.

"For the charity gala," he said.

She'd hoped he'd forgotten. "Oh, that. I'm going to volunteer, so I actually need to be there early. I can just meet—"

He shook his head. "No. It won't be a problem. I can pick you up early. What time works best for you?"

Emma barely resisted the urge to squirm. Showing up with Damien would be like linking herself with the enemy. She narrowed her eyes, wondering if he were doing this precisely to make her squirm. But what choice did she have? "Five-thirty should be fine," she said, preparing herself for disapproving expressions from the De Luca and Megalos couples. "I promised Mallory I would assist with any last-minute problems. I understand if you want to bow out since my attention will be divided."

"I wouldn't think of it," he said, his dark eyes glinting with determination.

She swallowed a sigh. "I'll see you then," she said, and turned.

"One other thing," he said, and she turned back around.

"Yes?"

"I've been asked to review a property in South Beach that MD wants to purchase."

She nodded. "Yes?"

"You and I are going there next week to review the

property in person," he said, as if he was informing her that she would be joining him at a business luncheon in a diner.

She stared at him in disbelief.

"You need to call my private jet. We'll leave on Wednesday and return on Sunday. I'll make the hotel reservations under a different name so they won't know they're being observed."

She nodded, stunned by the news, but determined to keep her composure. "Okay. You'll give me the number," she said. "For your private jet?"

He scribbled it on a piece of paper and handed it to her. "There it is. Pack like a tourist. Swimsuits, dresses. No business attire required." He handed her a credit card. "Buy everything you need and put it on my card."

"Oh, that's not necessary. I have dresses. I have a swimsuit," she said, remembering she'd bought one at a discount store three years ago…or was it four?

"We're going in disguise," he said. "I'll book adjoining suites, but we'll be a couple. Use my card. I want you to dress the part. Dress like my woman would."

Six

Although she'd bought it on sale, Emma spent more than she would have preferred on a black full-length gown with a discreet halter top that plunged in the back. Stepping into kitten-heel sandals, she grabbed the small beaded clutch she'd bought at her favorite thrift store and checked the mirror once more. With smoky eyes, shiny lip gloss and her hair swinging free to her shoulders, she almost didn't recognize herself. She looked almost glamorous.

She hoped she didn't look as if she were trying too hard. For the fifth time, she thought about ditching the dress, scrubbing off her makeup and calling in sick. Calling in sick, however, was something she'd never done in her life, and she refused to start now.

The doorbell rang, and she nearly jumped out of her skin. Taking a deep breath to calm herself, she walked to the door and opened it. She looked at Damien, dark and dangerous in a black tux. The breath she'd just taken stuck in her throat.

He seemed taller, she thought, and the way he looked at her made her stomach dip and sway.

"You look beautiful," he said, extending his hand.

"Thank you," she said, reluctant to take his hand, fearing she might get burned just by the sensation of his skin on hers. Crazy, she thought, and took his hand. "You look very nice, too," she said in a brisk tone that sounded at odds with her compliment, even to herself.

She was thankful the sun was still shining to help her ward off any forbidden fantasies her mind might conjure. She blinked at the sight of a driver holding the door to a limo. "I didn't expect—"

"I couldn't have you crawling out of a Ferrari when you're dressed for a ball."

He helped her into the limo and followed her inside.

"Thank you," she murmured, feeling like Cinderella. She'd ridden in a limo before, but she'd been taking notes from Alex Megalos during the drive.

"Something to drink?" he asked, waving his hand toward the bar.

"Oh, no, thank you," she said and took another deep breath, inhaling a hint of his cologne. The silence inside the limo was deafening. She supposed she should try to make small talk, but she was too aware of the fact that his thigh was mere inches from hers.

"Have you had a chance to go shopping for our trip?" he asked, adjusting one of the cuffs of his shirt.

Distracted by the contrast of his white shirt against his tanned skin, she again noticed the bandage around his hand. "How is your hand?"

"I don't pay much attention to it. The stitches will be out next week."

"Good," she said.

"You didn't answer my question," he said with a hint of amusement in his deep voice.

She met his gaze. "Shopping," she echoed and shook her head. "No. I haven't had a chance. Maybe tomorrow."

"You don't sound very enthusiastic," he said.

"I'm not comfortable using company money for my wardrobe, especially when I know job cuts are on the way."

"It's not Megalos-De Luca money. It's my company's money, and trust me, we're not hurting." He shook his head. "I'm surprised. Most women would jump at the chance."

Most women weren't her. "With my background, being thrifty was necessary for my survival. You should understand that from your own experiences."

"True," he said. "But I can loosen the purse strings when necessary."

"I'm definitely not at your level and I always feel as if I need to be prepared—" She broke off, not wanting to reveal the rest.

"Prepared for what?" he asked.

"The worst," she said.

He nodded. "Something we have in common. Who knows," he said, his gaze falling over her with sensual curiosity. "There may be more."

As Emma and Damien entered the grand ballroom at the casino, Emma caught the expression of shock and confusion on Mallory's face.

"Emma," Alex Megalos's wife said, clearly searching for words.

"Hi, Mallory. Have you met Damien? He's working for Megalos-De Luca. Apparently he hasn't had a chance to get out much since he's been in Vegas, so he asked if he could come with me and drop a bundle at the gala tonight."

Mallory blinked, still confused, but game. "How generous of you, Mr. Medici. You may not remember me. I'm—"

"How could I forget you," Damien said, taking her hand and lifting it to his lips. "You are the enchanting wife of Alex Megalos."

Mallory smiled, but she didn't appear to buy his charm. "Thank you. And thank you for contributing to the success of our charity gala tonight. Your donation will mean a lot to us. I hope you don't mind if I borrow Emma for a bit. We have some last-minute tasks," she said and grabbed Emma's hand.

"Just make sure you return her to me," he said, looking at Emma.

"Oh, count on it," Mallory said and pulled Emma away.

Mallory dragged Emma across the ballroom and into a back room. She pushed Emma against the wall, her eyes wide with consternation. "What the—"

"He insisted on joining me. I'd just been in Alex's office telling him—" She shrugged "—giving a report and Mr. Medici showed up at the elevator just as I was leaving. I tried to discourage him, but no luck."

Mallory shook her head. "Wow. Do you think he's interested in you?"

"Oh, no," Emma said, feeling herself grow warm. "I'm sure he's got another agenda. He's that kind of man," she said, giving voice to what was always in the back of her mind.

Mallory's eyebrows shot upward. "Sounds like you're getting to know him pretty well."

Emma winced. "Not really. Not as much as I'm supposed—" She broke off again, because she didn't know how much Alex had told his sweet bride. "So," she said as brightly as she could. "Tell me how I can help."

Mallory frowned. "Are you okay?"

"Uh-huh," Emma said, quickly composing herself. She wondered why it was so easy with Mallory and so difficult with Damien. "Are you?"

Mallory gave a start. "Well, yes. So how was your date last week?"

"He was very nice."

Mallory's face fell. "Okay, I get your message.

We'll move along to bachelor number two. Is next Tuesday good?"

"Let's try the week after. Next week is busy for me," she said, her heart skipping a beat when she thought about the trip to Miami. Should she tell Max or Alex? Why did she feel so conflicted? Emma shook off her craziness. "I'm waiting. How can I help?"

Mallory paused for a moment, then nodded. "We got some last-minute big rollers and they've totally messed up my seating arrangements. Help."

Emma smiled. Now she was on familiar ground. "Give me the list."

Damien took a seat at the bar and ordered a scotch. Struck by the sumptuous luxury of the ballroom, he couldn't help remembering that lean time when he'd been declared an independent child and lived hand to mouth. Even before his father had died, his family had never been wealthy. They'd never owned their own home.

He caught sight of an advertisement on the wall for Megalos-De Luca proudly announcing their charitable contributions and felt bitterness roil through him like acid. The irony of the De Luca family being the least bit connected to anything charitable was a joke.

When Damien thought about how the De Lucas had cheated his grandfather out of the Medicis' beloved estate, the fire roared inside him again. The once solid family had scattered, and were still scattered. One of his uncles had committed suicide, an aunt betrothed to a prince had been dumped. Children had been orphaned. Someone had to make this right. That someone was him.

Emma caught his eye as she passed him by. She glided with confidence through the ballroom and smiled at the waitstaff in a much friendlier, more open way than she did him. That fact stuck in his craw. He wondered what it would be like if she were that open with him. He felt an odd growl in his gut and watched her through narrowed eyes. Why should it bother him?

He would have her. In every way a man could have a woman, he was determined to have her, and he would. He took another swallow of whiskey and felt the burn all the way down. Not only would she give him herself, she would give him all the information he wanted to make Max De Luca pay.

"What do you want to drink?" Damien asked her as he played blackjack at the charity high-roller table.

Emma noticed he was winning against the house. No surprise there. "I don't drink very often. I'm always the DD."

"No need tonight," he said. "A limo will safely transport you home."

She met his gaze and felt the frisson of something between them. How could that be? He was the devil. The obscenely wealthy devil and she, well, she was just Emma. "Something with peach schnapps," she admitted in a low voice, leaning toward him. "A lady's drink."

"Got it," he said and turned to the waitress in the ultra-short black dress. "Sex on the Beach," he said. "Water for me."

Emma frowned at him and he lifted his hands. "Hey, I'm gambling," he said. "I have to keep my head."

"Does winning matter that much?" she asked as the dealer shuffled the deck for another game. "Since the money goes to charity anyway."

He gave a low, dirty chuckle and shook his head. "Winning always matters," he said.

Sipping her fruity drink, Emma watched him rack up the chips until it appeared he'd accumulated a mountain of them. "I'll cash them in now," he finally said to the dealer and rose from the table.

"That's a lot of money," she said after he cashed in his chips and collected a receipt for charity.

"It's deductible." He shot her a sideways glance. "Plus I had to deliver on your promise to Mallory that I was going to drop a bundle."

Emma fought a twist of discomfort. It had been presumptuous of her to promise Damien's money. On the other hand, it had been presumptuous of Damien to insist on attending the event with her.

"Don't worry. I know you were protecting me," he said.

"Protecting you," she echoed in disbelief. "Why would I do that? Why would you of all people need protection?"

"Because Mallory Megalos wanted to scratch off my face."

"I can't believe you would be concerned by Mallory."

"I'm not. I learned long ago not to rely on anyone's opinion but my own, but it's good to know you were looking out for my best interests."

His comment was so far from the truth it was all she could do not to correct him. She remembered, however, that it was part of her goal to get him to trust her so that she could get information for Alex and Max.

Managing a tight smile, she glanced at the buffet and moved toward it. "After all that gaming, I bet you're hungry. See anything you like?"

"Yes, I do," he said in a low, intimate voice that snagged her attention. She looked at him and his gaze was focused totally on her. She felt a rush of heat. "The food does look delicious," she said, attempting to distract him.

His gaze didn't budge. "Delicious," he said, but he clearly wasn't referring to the food.

Emma felt as if she needed a fan.

A hand brushed her back and she turned to find Doug Caldwell, her blind date from the previous night. "It's good to see you. Mallory didn't tell me you were coming tonight."

"Probably because I was going to be helping her. Damien Medici, this is Doug Caldwell."

"Good to meet you," Doug said. "You don't mind if I borrow Emma for a dance, do you?"

Wearing an inscrutable expression, Damien remained silent for a long, uncomfortable moment.

Doug gave an uneasy laugh. "Just one," he promised. "Unless you're engaged."

"Of course not," Emma replied. "Excuse me and enjoy the buffet."

Inwardly fuming, she allowed Doug to guide her onto the dance floor.

"Who is that guy, anyway?" Doug asked.

"My boss," she said and watched him lift his eyebrows. "Well, not exactly my boss. I've been assigned to work with him while he performs a service for the company."

"He seemed territorial about you. Maybe he's interested in more than business."

"Oh, no. He's just one of those men who come across as intimidating the first time you meet him." And the second time, and the third....

"If that's the case and you're up for it, I'd like to take you to dinner next weekend."

She wasn't, but she also didn't want Doug to think anything romantic was happening between her and Damien. "I wish I could, but I'm going to be out of town next weekend."

"Then how about the weekend after that?"

"My schedule is tight right now, but maybe we could meet for cocktails again."

"I was hoping for something more," he said.

"I'm sorry. I'm taking some classes, so I'm very busy."

He gave a put-upon sigh. "Okay, I'll take what I

can get. Cocktails on Saturday night in two weeks. Don't forget."

She nodded and the music stopped, saving her from further discussion. Just a few feet after parting with Doug, she felt a warm, strong hand close over hers and looked up to find Damien.

"Hello," she said, taken off guard, distracted by the sensation of his closeness.

"My turn," he said and as another song began, he pulled her into his arms.

She quickly glanced over her shoulder, wondering who was watching. "Are you sure this is a good idea? I wouldn't want to start rumors."

"I've never been bothered by rumors. Are you worried that all the MD people are going to think you're making nice to the hatchet man?"

She gasped at his bluntness. "I've always made it a practice to keep my professional relationships completely professional."

"You're telling me you weren't attracted to your previous bosses," he said.

Feeling his crisp tuxedo jacket beneath her hand, she couldn't help wondering how his naked shoulder would feel. How would his skin feel? She tried to squelch her curiosity. "Well, I didn't mean to say they're not attractive men. They are and they're very good men, but my relationships with my bosses have always been work-focused."

"But they didn't affect you like I do."

Her breath stopped in her throat. She swallowed hard.

"You're not denying it," he said.

Emma grasped for her usual rational, cautious mind. "Just because there's some sort of odd, fleeting, marginal chemistry doesn't mean anyone should act on it."

He lifted a dark eyebrow. "Marginal, fleeting," he echoed.

"Exactly," she said, wishing her heart wasn't racing so fast. "Chemistry is just chemistry."

"One of the things I noticed about MD is that they don't have a policy against employees fraternizing with each other."

"Yes, but fraternization just muddies the water." And the mind, she thought, determined to keep her own mind clear as the sound of a saxophone oozed through the room.

"You don't need to be afraid," he said.

"What do you mean?"

"I would never force you. I've never had to force a woman." He leaned closer, brushing his mouth just an inch from her ear. "You would come to me."

Fighting his knee-weakening effect on her, she pulled back. "I'm not that easily seduced," she whispered.

"I never said you were easy," he told her. "I just said there was something between us. Not the usual attraction. At some point, we're going to need to explore it to get past it. We may as well enjoy it."

Part of her may have felt he was right, but she refused to give into it. She stepped backward. "We won't have an affair. I won't come to you. Count on it," she said and turned away. Florida was going to be oh-so-great, she thought as she stalked toward the bar to get a bottle of water. She might as well be walking through hell.

Later that evening, Mallory Megalos announced the winners of the raffle items. One person won a vacation to Greece, another to Italy, another to France. Someone else won a sports car. Emma wasn't paying attention to the names of the winners because she hadn't entered any of the drawings. With her mother's problems, she never gambled.

"The winner of the Tesla Roadster, with taxes absorbed by an anonymous donor, is Emma Weatherfield," Mallory announced.

"Emma!" a coworker exclaimed.

She snapped her head around to meet the manager's excited gaze. "Excuse me?"

"You just won a car."

Emma frowned. "That's not possible. I didn't enter. I didn't buy any raffle tickets..."

"Emma, you won a Tesla Roadster," Mallory announced from the platform. "Come and get the keys."

Confused, she shot a quick glance around her and walked toward the platform. "I'm sorry," she whispered to Mallory. "There must be some mistake. I didn't buy any tickets."

"Well, someone must have entered your name,"

Mallory said, lifting the ticket with her name scrawled on it. "This is the coolest car in the world. I would be jealous if Alex didn't let me drive his."

"How—"

"Congratulations, Emma Weatherfield!" Mallory said.

Still disbelieving, she reluctantly accepted the keys. "Thank you. Thank you so much." Glancing into the crowd, she caught sight of Damien. He wore a mysterious yet knowing expression on his face, and she immediately suspected he was behind her win. She also knew she couldn't accept the car.

Seven

Emma pressed the keys into Damien's hand as he assisted her into the waiting limo.

Following her inside the car, he looked down at the keys. "What's this?"

"Those are the keys to the car that you won from the raffle tonight," she said.

"Couldn't be mine. I didn't enter the raffle." He extended his arm to drop them into her lap. "I'm not big on counting on luck."

"I didn't enter the raffle, either. The tickets were too expensive. Twenty-five dollars each," she said, her frustration rising. "It had to be you."

"Why?" he asked. "Don't you have other friends and

admirers? Couldn't someone else have just decided to buy several tickets and put names of friends on them?"

Emma studied his face, her gaze sliding to the scar. The mark of imperfection was incredibly sexy to her and the fact that she knew he'd gotten that scar protecting someone got to her every time she looked at his face. She tried to read his expression, but it was inscrutable.

Narrowing her eyes, she shook her head. "Something about this is fishy. I almost feel as if I should give the car back."

He lifted his eyebrows. "I wasn't aware that your current mode of transportation was in such great condition that you could throw away a brand-new car."

"Well, a roadster isn't very practical," she countered.

"True. It's only a two-seater. You don't have children, do you?"

"You know I don't," she said. "But there's also not a lot of space for packing things in the trunk."

He nodded. "You take a lot of driving trips?"

"Not really," she admitted. "But I do visit my mother in Missouri sometimes."

"I hear it will go two hundred and twenty miles on one charge," he said casually.

"I know all about the specs. I was in charge of making sure Alex Megalos got his the first possible second."

"Nice company car," Damien said in a tone brimming with disapproval.

"The company didn't pay for the car," she quickly

told him. "He paid for it out of his own money. Which leads me back to my original point. I didn't buy a raffle ticket, so how could I have won it?"

"Apparently someone entered for you," he said. "Someone wanted you to have the car."

She frowned, crossing her arms over her chest. "I'm not comfortable with this at all."

"Many people aren't comfortable with change," he said.

She glanced at him again, wondering if he was talking about the changes that would be taking place within MD. Or other possible personal changes. Her gaze dipped involuntarily to his mouth and she felt an unbidden rush of warmth. She forced her gaze away, but was still aware of him, the scent of his cologne, the closeness of his body. His hip was mere inches from hers. She glimpsed his long legs in her peripheral vision. His hand rested on the leather seat just above her shoulder.

He confused her. If he was trying to buy her loyalty or something else, wouldn't he have taken credit for entering her in the lottery and held it over her head?

She turned toward him, looking up into his face. "If some mystery person had bought a lottery ticket on your behalf and you'd won, what would you do?"

"I don't have personal experience. No one has ever bought a lottery ticket on my behalf," he said in a dry tone. "I've had offers for free headstone markers—"

"You haven't received death threats?" she asked, feeling a chill.

"Too many to count, but that wasn't your original question. If I won a car and liked it, I would keep it. If I'd won this car and didn't want it, I would sell it because the demand for the car is so high."

"Sell it," she echoed. "That sounds almost mercenary considering I got it because of a charity drive."

"If you sell it, you could buy yourself a new car and put the rest of the cash in the bank."

The idea tempted her. "If I bought a good used car…"

"I didn't suggest you go that far," he said. "If you insist on selling it, the least you can do is get yourself new, reliable transportation."

She threw him a sideways glance. "Considering you didn't enter the lottery for me, you seem to have a strong opinion."

"You asked my opinion."

True, she thought.

"Do you like the car?"

"I haven't even driven it yet. I was told it could be delivered as soon as Monday. I don't even know how to drive the thing."

"I'm sure the person who delivers it will be glad to show you." He paused a moment. "You could wait to make your decision after you've taken the car for a ride. It's often wise not to judge before you've had a chance to evaluate the car for yourself."

His gaze held hers and she couldn't help comparing him to a fast, dangerous sports car. *What kind of ride would he give?* Emma should have been horrified by the direction of her thoughts, but when he lowered his fingers to brush back a strand of her hair, all she could do was stare.

He lowered his head and she held her breath. *Was he going to kiss her?* She should turn away, push him away, but she couldn't move.

"It's your call, Emma. No one is going to force you. You can give the keys back before, or you can take a ride and decide for yourself."

His voice was low and intimate, the same way he would talk to a lover. She felt an ache start in her breasts and slide lower into her nether regions. She couldn't remember feeling this aroused by a man, and he'd barely touched her. What if he'd kissed her? Would she be able to resist him? Would she want to?

The limo pulled to a stop, distracting her. Glancing out the window, she saw that they had arrived at her apartment's parking lot. She cleared her throat and decided to say goodbye here before he made her have another sensual meltdown. "Well, thank you for your generous contribution to charity this evening."

"I'll walk you inside," he said and gave the chauffeur a quick nod. The chauffeur opened the door. Damien got out and extended his hand to help her.

"It's really not necessary," she said.

"I insist," he said, and she knew it was useless to argue.

She released his hand as quickly as possible, but the sidewalk was too small. With each step, her bare shoulder brushed against his arm. Determined to escape him as soon as possible, she pushed her key into the door lock and turned it, glancing over her shoulder. "Again, thank you for—"

The door whisked open, taking her off guard. Her mother stepped into view. "Surprise! I found a deal on a flight and took an extra day off. I've been missing my baby girl."

"Mother," she said, surprised, noting that her mother had changed her hair color again. Violet-red this time. "How did you—"

"I have to go back on the red-eye on Monday night, but it was worth it. It's been too long," her mother said, then glanced past Emma to Damien. Her blue eyes rounded. "Oh, my, I've interrupted a date. You actually went on a date." She craned her neck to get a better look. "Is that a limo? Why didn't you tell me?"

Emma felt a rush of embarrassment. "This wasn't a date. It was a charity gala. This is my boss, Damien Medici."

Her mother's eyebrows sprang upward and she pursed her lips into an O.

Damien extended his hand. "It's a pleasure to meet you, Ms.?"

Her mother glanced at Emma. "What nice manners. My name is Kay Nelson. And it's my pleasure to meet you. I don't usually get to meet Emma's coworkers, so this is a treat."

"He's not a coworker," Emma quickly said. "He's my boss."

"Oh," Kay said. "Well, would you like to come

inside? I brought Emma a bottle of wine and baked her favorite cookies as part of her surprise."

Emma stared at her mother in dismay. "Oh, no, I'm sure Mr. Medici is too—"

"I'd love to," he said, and Emma swallowed an oath.

Damien wouldn't dare give up this golden opportunity to get a different view of Emma outside work. Her mother was a charming, but fidgety, little magpie. She seemed unable to sit for more than a few minutes before jumping up for one reason or another. "Would you like more wine, Damien?" she asked.

He held up his hand at her offer of the pink beverage. He'd managed to swallow a few sips for the sake of being sociable, but he preferred dry red wine to white and never, ever pink.

"I'm sure you can imagine how proud I am of Emma. She's always been a good girl. Much more conservative than I am, and look at her now. Working at Megalos-De Luca. Do you know she has worked for two vice presidents?"

"Yes, Mother, he knows," Emma said.

"Well you can't blame me for bragging about you. That gown is just beautiful. You've done something different with your hair, too, haven't you?"

"Mother," Emma said. "I think Mr. Medici needs to leave."

"There's no need to rush," her mother protested. "Do you need to leave, Damien? If you're worried about running up the bill with the limo sitting out there, I'm sure Emma would be happy to drive you home."

Emma's mouth dropped open in protest.

"I'm in no rush," Damien said, leaning back in his chair, ignoring Emma's hostile glare. "Tell me more about Emma as a child."

"She was so thrifty. I swear that girl could make a penny squeal." Kay sighed. "But you know we didn't always have it easy, so that was a good thing. I nick-named her Goddess Hestia. Can you guess why?"

"That's the goddess of hearth and home, right?"

"Yes," Kay said. "We moved a lot and Emma was quick to make anywhere we lived into a home. What a life. Remember the pony I got for you that Christmas?"

Emma nodded with a soft smile. "Peanut."

"She loved that pony. Unfortunately we ran into a little difficulty and could only keep him for a year."

Emma's smile turned strained. "That was one of the good years," she said.

"She always loved animals. What was the name of the last dog we had?"

"Sheba, a golden retriever. We had to give her away because we moved to a place that didn't allow pets."

"I'm surprised you don't have a pet now that you're on your own," Damien said.

"I'm gone too much. It wouldn't be fair."

"Always practical," Kay said, lifting her hands. "Too busy to date in high school. Too busy to do much dating at all. I'm happy you went out tonight."

"It wasn't a date, Mom," Emma said, standing as if she couldn't bear the conversation one minute longer. "Thank you again, Damien."

He rose to his feet. "My pleasure," he said. "Perhaps your mother can help you shop for your upcoming trip."

"Trip," Kay said, immediately perking up. "What trip?"

"I'm going on a business trip to South Beach to evaluate one of the resorts down there. I'll be buying a few new things because I'll be posing as a resort guest."

"I've told her to put it on my account," Damien said.

"Oh, my, how generous. South Beach is so romantic. I went there once with my third husband." She frowned. "Or was it my fourth?"

"Your third," Emma said in a low voice and moved swiftly to the front door. "Oh, my goodness, look at the time. We didn't mean to keep you so long, Damien."

"Oh," Kay said, jumping from her perch on the sofa. "I should leave so the two of you can say good-night privately."

Emma's eyes rounded in horror. "No." She barely got out the word before her mother disappeared into a back room. "I apologize for my mother. She means well."

"I found her charming," he said. "And I wouldn't want to disappoint her by not saying good-night to you privately," he added, stepping so close to her it was all he could do not to take her into his arms, all he could do not to take her mouth and slide his tongue over hers so she wouldn't be able to deny the heat between them any longer.

Damien knew, however, that Emma would have to come to him. It would take every ounce of his self-control, but it was necessary. He lowered his head, closer and closer. Her eyes fluttered and he heard the soft intake of her breath. He moved his mouth so close he could feel her breath. Her body hummed with expectation. Her eyes fluttered again.

It would be all too easy to pull her against his chest, to kiss her every objection away. He wanted to strip her of her reserve and poise until she was begging for him. To fill his hands with her breasts and explore all her secrets. He would tease her until she called out his name again and again. Then he would thrust inside her and give them both the satisfaction they craved.

Hard with desire, he fought against temptation.

"Good night, Goddess Hestia," he said. Then he walked away.

It took a full moment of the cool night air drifting over her skin where Damien had been radiating heat just seconds earlier before she realized he'd left. And he hadn't kissed her. Her body screamed in protest. Her nipples were taut buds straining against her dress and she was wet with wanting.

Chagrined by her response, she forced herself into her apartment with one last glance at the taillights of the limo as it left her parking lot. She felt like an idiot. She'd practically melted into the doorjamb.

She should be relieved that he hadn't kissed her. It would have been completely unprofessional. Instead, she was peeved. How could he get so close to her, nearly rubbing his body against hers, close enough to give her the kind of kiss that sent rockets around the world, and not touch her?

A strangled groan escaped from her throat just as her mother entered the room. "Oh, sweetheart, I'm so sorry. Did you have a romantic evening planned with Damien? I hope I didn't interrupt."

Emma couldn't quite swallow another groan. *"He's my boss, Mother. Nothing more."*

Her mother shook her head. "He is gorgeous and he clearly thinks a lot of you. There's no reason you shouldn't enjoy yourself with him. Trust me, you don't meet men like him every day."

"I'm aware of that, but—"

"I mean I can see why you might find his facial scar frightening. It does look a little savage and—"

"He was defending his foster mother when he got that scar."

Her mother lifted her eyebrows. "Oh. It sounds like the two of you have gotten to know each other quite well considering he's *just your boss.*"

Emma sighed. "Can we please talk about something else? Like when did you decide to visit me?"

"I know I'm imposing, but I've missed you."

"You're not imposing," Emma said, putting her

arms around her mother and giving her a hug. "You know I'm always happy to see you. But I do like a little notice so I can meet you at the airport."

"To make sure I don't stop at the slot machines," her mother said. "Don't worry. I resisted temptation."

"I'm proud of you."

"Thank you, baby. I wish I could be closer to you. Missouri is so slow compared to Vegas."

"Peaceful," Emma corrected. "Remember, when you first moved there, you said it was peaceful. How's Aunt Julia?"

"She's doing fine. She loves her grandbabies. I would love to have some of my own," her mother hinted.

"Not for a long time," Emma muttered. "I'm really tired. I'll fix you banana pancakes in the morning. Would you like that?"

"You're so good to me," her mother said. "You've been making banana pancakes for me since that Mother's Day when you were eleven years old."

"Eight," Emma said, smiling at the memory. "But who's counting?"

"After breakfast, we can go shopping," her mother said. "I can't wait. Sweetie, this time you don't even need to look for sales since it's not your money."

The next morning, after Emma made banana pancakes with real maple syrup for her mother, the two of them went shopping.

"We can go to the Versace store," her mother said.

"Hmm," Emma said.

"Louis Vuitton," her mother continued, rapturous. "Roberto Cavalli."

Or not, she thought as she pulled into an outlet mall.

"Darling," her mother said. "Why are we going to an outlet mall when you could shop at any designer store in Vegas?"

"Because I'm not using Damien Medici's money," Emma said, delighted to find a parking space close to an entrance.

"But he offered. I'll bet he even insisted. Why do you deprive yourself this way?" her mother asked.

Emma didn't want to remind her mother of all the times they'd overspent only to have to return the luxury items they'd purchased. She didn't want to tell her mother that she still lived in fear that her mother would gamble again, fall into debt, leaving Emma to cover the losses.

"This is like a hunting expedition," she told her mother. "You and I are looking for several prize animals." Emma watched her mother, seeing something click in her gaze.

"You like the challenge of bagging the big one on your own terms. I'm in," her mother said, and got outside the car, her tennis-shoe-clad feet ready to pound hard, unforgiving floors for the prizes that awaited them.

Eight

Thank goodness Damien was out of the office during most of Monday and Tuesday. He sent a town car to collect her on Wednesday morning. The driver opened the car door for her to slide onto a luxurious leather seat while he loaded her luggage into the trunk.

Emma's heart pounded, but she told herself to be calm. Damien had proven that he wouldn't force himself on her. If he could control himself, then she should be able to control herself.

She hoped she had the right clothes. Her mother had insisted on several purchases that Emma wouldn't normally have chosen. Emma had agreed to them only because her mother had visited South Beach and she hadn't.

Currently dressed in designer jeans, a silk tank top and crocheted sweater to keep her warm during the flight, she bit her lip, trying not to feel insecure. She pumped her foot, idly noticing her wedge-heel sandals and pearl and sterling silver anklet. She hoped she looked touristy enough.

Damien was probably accustomed to being surrounded by women who dropped thousands of dollars on revealing clothes without batting an eye. Emma couldn't imagine ever being that kind of woman. Instead of going to the main terminal, the driver took an alternate route. She glanced at her watch, worried that he may put her behind schedule.

"Excuse me," she said. "Don't we need to go to the main terminal?"

The driver shook his head. "No, Ma'am. Different terminal. You're flying on a private jet."

"Oh," she said, leaning back in her seat. Soon enough, he pulled in front of another terminal and unloaded her luggage. Her walk through security was effortless and quick. Afterward, she followed an attendant to a corporate jet and boarded.

"We'll be leaving very soon," the attendant told her. "What can I get you to drink? Juice, water?"

"Water would be fine," she said, glancing past the woman and spotting Damien. She felt a kick in her stomach.

He glanced up from his paperwork and shoved it aside. He stood. "Prompt as ever," he said with a slight smile.

She walked toward him, feeling an odd sense of relief at his presence. "I forgot we weren't going to the main terminal."

"I fly commercially sometimes, but more for trips to Europe, Asia or Australia. This is one of my indulgences," he confessed. "I like traveling on my own timetable. I can get more work done in a more comfortable environment." He smiled in a conspiratorial way. "See. I don't have to chew glass to be happy."

She couldn't swallow a laugh.

"There you go," he said. "You're not a nervous flyer."

She shook her head. "Not unless there's a lot of turbulence."

"I'll tell the pilot to avoid it," he said.

"Is that like fries?" she asked. "I'd like a burger with fries. I'd like a smooth flight with no turbulence."

He chuckled. "I never thought of it that way, but yes, maybe. Have a seat. Are you hungry? Thirsty?"

"The attendant already asked me what I wanted to drink," she said, sitting down. At that moment, the perky attendant brought out chilled bottled water for both Emma and Damien, and juice for Damien.

"Would you like breakfast?" he asked her.

"I grabbed a bagel before I left home."

He nodded. "I'll take my regular," he said and sat down.

Curious, she leaned toward him as she sat across from him. "What's your regular?"

"Breakfast is two scrambled eggs, bacon, whole wheat toast, grape jam and breakfast potatoes."

"Lunch?"

"If I take it, club on whole wheat, salt and vinegar chips, dill spear."

"Dinner?"

"Filet mignon, rare, baked potato, broccoli, Caesar salad. Scotch."

"You reward yourself if you have to travel at night," she said.

"Damn right."

"I've learned more about your diet in the last two minutes than I have the entire time I've worked for you," she said.

"Some people say that flying eliminates boundaries that concrete emphasizes."

"In what way?"

"You're secluded above the atmosphere with one other person. No distractions unless you invent them. No interruptions. Just time with little space separating you from that one other person," he said.

The expression in his gaze sent a montage of hot visuals through her mind. This was way too early in the morning and during the trip for her to be thinking about Damien…that way. Taking a quick breath, she deliberately tried to break the hum between them that seemed to grow louder with each passing second.

"Except when you're stuck in the center seat with a child on either side of you," she said.

He chuckled. "That's when noise-canceling ear-phones are required."

"That won't stop bathroom trips and spills," Emma said.

"You say that as if you have experience," he said.

"I do. I've had to take a few last-minute flights that were packed."

"None of that today," he said.

Emma relaxed slightly into her leather seat. "So true."

The attendant peeked into the lush passenger area. "The pilot says we're ready for takeoff. Please fasten your seat belts."

A few hours later, the jet landed in Miami and a limo pulled alongside the plane. Although Emma had made the travel arrangements herself, she couldn't help but appreciate the efficiency. Within forty-five minutes, they'd checked into the resort they were to evaluate, and she was wandering around her private suite located next door to Damien's. The lavish suite featured a sitting area with a wall of windows that opened onto a balcony that overlooked the resort's three pools, Jacuzzis and the turquoise ocean. She took a deep breath of the ocean air and enjoyed the breeze as it played over her skin. Hard to believe this was *work*.

"What do you think so far?" a voice said from the balcony beside her.

She glanced over to find Damien looking at her.

He'd already changed out of his business clothes and wore a tight black T-shirt that emphasized his broad shoulders and well-developed chest and biceps. She couldn't seem to stop her gaze from following down the rest of his body to lean hips encased in swim trunks. Her mouth went dry and she licked her lips. What had he asked her?

"Pardon me?" she said in a voice that sounded strained to her own ears.

"What do you think of the place so far?"

"It's beautiful. Check-in was smooth and the bellman was friendly. So far, my suite appears immaculate."

"Same here," he said. "It's almost as if they knew we were coming."

Emma felt a twist in her stomach. It was likely the staff had indeed known because she'd told Max about Damien's plans.

"We're just getting started. I haven't had time to review my checklist, but I will—"

"Later," he said. "We're burning daylight. Put on your swimsuit and meet me downstairs."

"Uh—" She started to protest because she had actually planned to conduct a thorough inventory of the suite, but he was the boss. "Okay. Give me just a few minutes," she said and walked inside the suite.

Even though Damien had been a perfect gentleman, she couldn't escape the barely hidden predatory watchfulness in his gaze. Try as she might, she couldn't ignore the simmering attraction between them.

Unpacking her swimsuit, Emma told herself she would just have to push her curiosity about Damien aside. Holding up the black string bikini her mother told her she must buy in order to fit in with the other tourists, Emma had second, third and fourth thoughts. Grabbing her sunscreen, oversize sunglasses, baseball cap and checklist, she told herself this was just business.

Damien lounged by the pool, responding to messages on his BlackBerry as he waited for Emma. He was counting on making this trip a turning point. By creating some distance between her and corporate headquarters, he planned to increase her sense of loyalty to him—mentally, physically and sexually.

Glancing upward, he spotted a pale woman wearing a baseball cap, huge sunglasses and a mesh cover-up that didn't conceal a tiny black bikini or the voluptuous body beneath it. Spotting her silky brown hair swinging over her shoulders, he realized it was Emma. Since she always hid herself beneath tailored suits, he'd only been able to imagine her naked.

Swearing under his breath, he took in every delicious inch of her. Her baby-pale skin would fry in this sun, he thought, immediately deciding to get an umbrella to shield her. Her full breasts bounced with each step. Her hips swayed invitingly.

Then she stopped suddenly as if she were looking

for him. He caught her nervousness as she licked her lips then bit her upper one. He withheld a groan while he mentally stripped her of those tiny pieces of fabric.

Damien stood and moved toward her. She immediately caught sight of him. "Hi," she said breathlessly. "It took me a little extra time because I had to put on sunscreen."

Damn shame, he thought. He would have loved to apply it himself. "No problem. I thought we'd go out to the beach since we don't have much time left today. We can check the pools and hot tubs later."

"Sure," she said and followed him to the towel hut. Holding the wooden door from the pool area for her, he took a lingering glance at her backside as she stepped in front of him.

Uh-huh. He had plans for her. They walked onto the beach and one of the beach staff approached them. "May I help you?"

"We'd like a cabana with two lounge chairs," Damien said.

"Right away, sir," the beach staff said and led them to a cabana, brushed sand off chairs and situated them underneath.

"Thank you," Emma said.

Damien nodded and tipped the man.

"Excellent service," she said, sitting down on the chair.

"Yes. Like I said, it's almost like they know they're being evaluated. But that couldn't be possible, could it?" he asked, studying her face.

She looked away. "Maybe they're always conscientious."

"Maybe," he agreed, but he already knew that Emma had informed Max about the trip. Ultimately, it wouldn't be his loss. It would be MD's loss because they wouldn't get an unbiased view of the resort. "Of course, here comes the cocktail waiter. What would you like?" he asked Emma.

"Something from the bar?" the waiter asked.

"I don't need anything. I brought water," she said, pulling a bottle from her bag and taking a sip.

"You must order something," he said. "How can you comment if you don't try everything?"

"You order for me, then."

"Beer for me and Sex on the Beach for the lady," he said and met her gaze dead-on.

Emma made a little choking sound. Damien took the opportunity to rub her back and gently squeeze one of her shoulders. "Okay?"

"Fine. Just fine," she said in a husky voice, leaning back in her chair. She covered her face with the cap from her head.

The waiter quickly filled the order and Damien drank half his beer while he urged Emma to polish off her mixed drink. He pulled off his T-shirt and baseball cap. "Would you like to go in the ocean?"

She sat up, but paused. "It's been a long time since I've been in the ocean."

"How long?"

"I live in Vegas, remember, so ten or more years."

He grabbed her hand. "Then we need to fix that right now," he said and led her toward the water.

"There's no rush," she said with a slight protest in her voice. "I don't have to do everything the first day."

"This isn't everything. This is just a little dip."

"Yes, but I think I might prefer the pool."

"It's been so long. How would you know?" he asked, tugging her into the surf.

"Whew! It's cool, isn't it?"

He smiled, finding her shyness appealing. "Are you afraid of the water?"

"Oh, no," she protested, but continued to grasp his hand like a vise.

"No problem. We can take it as slow as you want," he said, coming to a stop. He felt her gaze on him for a long moment, but couldn't read her expression because of her sunglasses.

"I can go a little further," she said in a low voice that had Damien visualizing her naked and beneath him again.

Oh, heaven help me, I'm standing next to Damien and he's half-naked. How in the world did he maintain that body? She shuddered at what he might think of her body. No one would call her reed-thin. A man like Damien must be accustomed to dating women with model-perfect figures.

Emma tried to push those thoughts from her head. It didn't matter if Damien thought she wasn't thin enough. In fact, it was all the better. With the cool water fluttering over her ankles, she stepped deeper into the ocean. The water splashed against her calves.

"Okay?" he asked, and she abruptly noticed that she was clasping his hand with a death grip.

"Oh," she said and tried to loosen her grip, but a wave took her by surprise. She gave a little jump.

He gave a low chuckle.

"Don't laugh at me," she scolded him and bit her lip as she forced herself to move forward. Another wave broke, licking at her thighs. She clasped his hand. "Are there jellyfish?"

"Probably not in May," he said.

"Probably," she echoed.

"I'll pick you up and carry you back if you see one," he offered.

Emma didn't know which prospect was worse— a jellyfish or being in Damien's arms. "Thanks," she muttered and inched forward. "Why do the waves seem to be getting bigger so quickly?"

"High tide," he said. "Do you want to go back?"

"Not yet," she said, refusing to give in to her fear. The last time she'd visited the ocean there'd been a strong undercurrent and she'd inhaled saltwater while she tried to determine which way was up. It wasn't a pleasant memory and she wanted to replace it with a better one. She walked further and the bottom seemed to fall out. Slipping into water up to her chin, she automatically clutched at Damien, wrapping her arms and legs around him. "What—" she gasped "—happened?"

"You're okay," he said, closing his strong arms around her. "We were on a sandbar and the bottom suddenly dipped. I've got you."

Surprisingly, the water was calmer. "Where did the waves go?" she asked.

"We're past them now," he said. "This is where it gets nice and calm. Do you like it?"

Taking in all the lovely sensations, she felt buoyant, yet protected. Her body had grown accustomed to the cooler temperature and she felt warm and safe against Damien's strong chest. Her legs dangled in the water while he made sure their heads stayed above the ocean.

She took a deep breath and something inside her eased. His skin was smooth beneath her fingers wrapped around the back of his neck. His chest glistened from the reflection of the sun.

"We should probably go back towards shore," she said, deferring to her logical, rational side.

"Yeah," he agreed. "Is that what you want?"

He felt deliciously strong and the sensation of the water washing over them was sensual in a way she'd never experienced. "Not really," she said, meeting his dark gaze. "It's nice."

"Yes, it is," he said, sliding his hands over her back. "Were you scared?"

"Nervous. It's been awhile and the last time I took a good dunking." She glanced out at the blue water, the sun making it sparkle like diamonds. "It's so beautiful."

"Have you ever been on a yacht?"

She shook her head. "No. Why?"

"My brother lives down here. He owns a yacht business."

She smiled. "Rough life."

He laughed. "That's what I say. Would you like to go for a ride?"

Intimately aware of the fact that he stood between her thighs, her breasts just below his chin, she already felt as if she were on a ride, a very dangerous one. "It's not part of our evaluation of the resort, is it?" she asked, but the idea of spending some time out on the water nearly made her drool.

"No, but we don't have to spend every minute evaluating the actual resort…"

"I'd love to," she said impulsively and hoped she wouldn't regret it later.

Nine

After a delicious dinner in the hotel's gourmet restaurant, Damien took Emma for a stroll down Lincoln Road to enjoy the night air and the outdoor mall. Emma had been a charming dinner companion, tasting and rating every dish. When she'd closed her eyes and licked her lips after sampling the chocolate cake, it had been all he could do not to carry her up to his room. "I've called my brother and he's taking us out on one of his yachts tomorrow. But you can go shopping the day after tomorrow while I'm catching up on some of my work. Use my card."

"Oh, I keep forgetting about your card," she said and abruptly stopped, her brown knee-length skirt swishing around her curvy legs. Her silk top emphasized her delicate shoulders and draped over her breasts. Damien was enjoying Emma's South Beach dress far more than her conservative office attire. She pulled out his credit card and held it toward him. "I don't need this anymore. Actually, I never did. I was able to find a few things on sale, so..."

"You didn't use my card?" he asked in disbelief.

She gave an uncomfortable shrug. "No. It just didn't seem—" She seemed to read his expression of disapproval. "I found bargains, so it wasn't necessary."

"I told you to use my card," he said, torn between dismay and anger. He'd never had a problem getting a woman to use his credit card for shopping before. "I knew you would need different clothing for this trip and it was appropriate for me to provide for that."

"I'll wear it again," she said.

"When?" he asked.

"Maybe on a date," she said, lifting her shoulders and smiling. "Mallory's determined to match me up with her friends."

Her reply irritated him. "So you'll wear that black bikini on a blind date?"

Her mouth opened and she paused before she closed it and bit her lip. "Well, maybe not, but I needed a new swimsuit anyway. Why is this such a problem? I was trying not to take inappropriate advantage."

Yet, she wouldn't bat an eye before betraying him to her former bosses. "It's insulting."

Her eyes widened. "I certainly didn't mean it that way." Her brow furrowed. "How could it be insulting?"

"I offered to provide clothing for a mandatory business trip and you rejected it."

"I apologize. I didn't look at it that way." She took a quick breath. "This trip has been wonderful so far. I just appreciate being able to be in this amazing place with—" She broke off suddenly as if she didn't want to finish the sentence. She didn't want to be happy being with *him*.

Another step closer, he realized with a sliver of satisfaction. He was making progress. Soon enough she would give him everything he wanted—her passion, and the information he needed to get De Luca. "Keep the card," he said. "Maybe you'll find something when you get a chance to go shopping. A souvenir."

After their walk, they returned to the hotel's night-club, which featured subdued lighting, white sheetlike drapes that extended from the high ceilings to the floor, couches and free-flowing martinis. A band played Cuban music, luring listeners onto the dance floor.

"I know Vegas has some hot nightspots, but like most natives I don't get out to them," Emma said as she sipped her martini. She glanced around. "There's something sybaritic about this place. How is your mojito?"

"A little sweet. I prefer my drinks dry. How is your martini?"

"Delicious and generous," she said. "After my full day, I'm almost afraid to drink it."

"It would be a shame to waste it," he said, looking at her mouth, wanting to taste it. The restless, irritable feeling inside him grew, but he tamped it down. "We should dance," he said.

"We should?" she echoed after taking another sip from her martini.

"We have to make our charade believable," he said and extended his hand. She followed him onto the dance floor and allowed him to pull her against his body.

The music shifted to a rhythm-and-blues tune and Damien decided, for once, to enjoy the moment. For just this song, he would steep himself in the scent and sensation of her and seduce her just a little further. Damien knew that anticipation was half the game.

He dipped his lips to her shoulder and glided them over her bare skin. She gave a delicate shiver, but didn't pull away. In fact, she lifted her arms and looped them around the back of his neck. Gratifying, he thought.

He slid his hand down to the small of her back and drew her intimately against him. Her breath caught, but still she didn't move away.

Every time she submitted to his physical approach, she bumped up his arousal another notch. He was already hard and allowed her to feel it.

He wanted nothing more than to take her mouth with his, but he waited. It killed him, but he waited, instead caressing her smooth neck. She felt pliant and willing in his arms. He decided to go a little further and slid his thigh between hers.

She gave a little whisper of a groan that intensified his arousal another degree. "Do you want me to kiss you?" he whispered against her ear.

She sighed, arching against him as if she wanted to be closer.

"If you want me to kiss you, lift your mouth," he told her, his voice sounding gritty with desire to his own ears. He waited and the seconds beat inside his head like a low-pitched bell that vibrated through his body. One, two, three…

She finally lifted her head, her eyes dark with need. "Kiss me," she whispered, and he lowered his head.

Her mouth felt like silk and satin and every sexy, soft thing he'd ever tasted. He lingered on her lips, savoring the sensation of her pliant mouth beneath his. Soon enough, though, it wasn't enough and he slid his tongue between the seam of her lips to taste her.

She gave a sexy little sigh, and allowed his entrance. She tasted sweet and forbidden. Her tongue wrapped around his, drawing him deeper. She may as well have been stroking him intimately for the effect she had on him. He couldn't remember a woman making him this hot. He wanted to touch all of her at once. Sliding his hand up her rib cage, just brushing the side of her breast, he continued to take her mouth.

She rubbed against him and he wanted to pull up her skirt so he could touch her sweetness. He wanted to drop his mouth to her breasts. Despite the fact that they were dancing in a darkened corner, he restrained himself.

"I want to put my mouth all over you," he muttered

against her mouth. "I want to taste you. I want to make you so hot you can't stand it and beg me for more. I want to slide deep inside you and fill you all the way."

She pressed her open mouth against his in sexual invitation. He kissed her once more, taking her mouth in only a fraction of the way he wanted to take her body. "There are beds with curtains by the pool. I could take you there."

"Oh," she said, taking in a quick, sharp breath. She met his gaze, her eyes full of wanting. "I don't know. It's so—"

"Decadent," he said. "Primal."

"Yes." She took another breath.

"It's up to you. I won't force you. I'm going outside to one of those beds. I have protection," he assured her. "We won't go any further than you want to go."

She licked her lips and he couldn't withhold a groan.

Her eyes widened at the sound. "I can't promise—"

"No promises," he said. "Just pleasure. I'll wait there for fifteen minutes," he said and pressed his mouth against hers before he walked away.

She would join him. He was confident of it. He should be feeling more of a sense of triumph. Especially for the larger goal of getting information from her. Instead, though, what he wanted more than anything was to feel her arms and legs wrap around him while he plunged inside her with nothing between them but skin and pounding blood. Damn, if he could explain it, but he wanted her affection and devotion, too.

* * *

Emma felt as if her brain had been scrambled. During the last three minutes, all her mental electrical circuits had fried to smithereens. "Come on, rational brain. Save me," she muttered as she glanced in the direction of the deserted beds by the pool. The beds featured curtains that shielded against prying eyes.

Damien Medici had just issued the wildest invitation she'd ever received in her life. Did she have the nerve to accept it? Perspiration dotted her forehead. Did she have the good sense and fortitude to turn him down or, if necessary, just run away to her suite upstairs?

Emma took another sip of the martini, despite the fact that she knew it wouldn't help clear her mind. Every fiber of her being craved Damien. She wanted to feel his skin against hers. She wanted him to make her moan. She wanted to make him groan.

If she followed her sensible self, she would run. It was insane.

It was also a once-in-a-lifetime opportunity.

She knocked back the rest of her martini and pushed aside her professional concerns. For the next hour or two, she wouldn't think about MD. She would think about Damien and her.

Walking toward the beds by the pool, she had second and third thoughts. She kept walking, though, glancing at the loungers, roped off from the crowd inside and on the patio. A little further and she began to feel uneasy. Perhaps she should go to her room.

Perhaps this was totally insane. It *was* totally insane, but maybe he was worth the insanity.

Emma walked past one more bed and felt the chicken in her start to squawk. Stopping, she took a deep breath and tried to calm herself. She felt her nerve begin to dissolve.

Maybe…

"Emma," Damien's voice, low, but strong, reached out to her. "I'm here."

Sucking in another deep breath, she slowly turned toward him. He stood just outside one of the poolside beds, the light outlining his tall, powerful frame.

Wanting washed over her. She wanted to be with him. She wanted to touch him. Gathering her nerve, she walked toward him. "I almost left," she confessed, looking into his face, half shielded by the darkness.

"I'm glad you didn't," he said and lifted his hand to her hair.

"Come inside," he coaxed.

With only his hand on her hair, she followed him inside, distantly aware of the swish of draperies closing behind her. The music from the live band played from a speaker in the pool area, adding to the sensuality of the atmosphere.

"Put your arms around me," he told her, and she did.

"This is crazy," she said, inhaling his scent from his open shirt.

"Yeah," he said, rubbing his forehead and nose against hers as he slid one hand underneath her hair and the other around the back of her waist. "Wanna stop?"

Her heart tripped over itself. "No," she whispered.

He pressed the small of her back, guiding her pelvis against his arousal. She felt herself grow hotter with each movement. The air inside the curtained area grew more steamy with each passing breath.

His movements were carnal and suggestive. She wasn't the least bit threatened, though. She wanted more. Lifting her head, she met his gaze and he guided her against him in a rhythm as old as time.

He swore, pulling her mouth against his and squeezing her bottom. Her heart raced and she felt light-headed. She had never felt this much want, this much need.

Tugging blindly at his shirt, she fumbled with his buttons. He pushed her hand aside and loosened them himself. She spread her hands over his warm, muscled flesh. So strong, so male.

His strength was an aphrodisiac. Distantly sensing his hands on the buttons of her blouse, she felt a draft of air on her back and her chest as her blouse dipped to her chest. One, two, three more seconds and her bra seemed to dissolve.

Her breasts meshed with his chest and she couldn't withhold a moan. He thrust his tongue into her mouth while he stroked the sides of her breasts. Her nipples peaked even though he hadn't touched them. Lower, she grew wet and swollen.

"So sweet, so good," he said, sliding his mouth down her throat, down her chest to her breast.

Emma held her breath, wanting, aching for more.

He gently pushed her back on the lush lounge and followed her down, taking one of her nipples into his mouth.

She arched toward him in pleasure and need. "Oh, Damien."

"I love the sound of my name on your lips," he muttered, sliding his lips down to her abdomen, pushing away her skirt. He skimmed his hand beneath her satin panties and found her most sensitive spot with unerring ease.

Emma shuddered at his intimate touch. She felt her body tighten with each stroke of his fingers, each breath that blew over her bare belly. He dipped lower and took her with his mouth.

Pleasured in a way she'd never experienced, she felt as if he were claiming her with his hands, with his mouth. Of its own volition her body shook with the beginning waves of climax.

Pulling away just before she soared, he skimmed his mouth back up her body. Every cell inside her was begging for him to finish her, to fill her up and take her the rest of the way. Her craving for him stole her breath.

"Inside," she said, clinging to his shoulders, drowning in his black gaze full of potent arousal. "Inside."

He pushed down his slacks and pulled on protection, then pushed her thighs apart. "Hold on tight," he said in a voice rough with need. Then he thrust inside her in one mind-blowing stroke.

He filled her, stretching her so that she could

barely catch her breath. The way he took her, the way he looked at her felt somehow primitive, as if he was laying claim to her and she would never be the same. Her heart pounding with overwhelming sensations and feelings, Emma couldn't tear her eyes from his. She lifted her hand to his face, touching his scar. He closed his eyes for a heartbeat, then rubbed his mouth over her hand.

He began to pump and the pleasure inside her quickly built again. The need edging toward desperation tightened. With each thrust, he took her higher and higher.

"I want it all, Emma. Give it all to me," he muttered.

His demand, his powerful thrusts and all the feelings she was experiencing were too much. Her body clenched him and a deep spasm of pleasure shot her into a realm of ecstasy she'd never experienced. A second later, he stiffened and swore, shuddering in climax. The experience was so powerful it took her a full moment to begin to breathe again.

Feeling his heartbeat pound against hers, she opened her eyes, half wondering if the earthquake that had taken place between them had brought down their outdoor boudoir if not the entire hotel.

She met his gaze to find him looking at her with an expression of primitive possession and a twinge of surprise. "I knew there was something between us, but—"

"It surprised me, too," she said, breathless.

"I want you to join me in my suite," he said and

pulled an extra key card from the pocket of his slacks as he got dressed. He handed her the key. "I want more time with you."

Taking his cue that it was time to get dressed, she gathered her wits, pulled on her clothes and slipped his key into her small purse. She met his gaze. "Is that an order?"

"Not at all," he said, leaning toward her and rubbing his mouth against hers. He arranged her blouse and smoothed her hair. The considerate gesture took her by surprise. "An invitation. You go first. I don't want to leave you here by yourself."

Her heart squeezed at his admission. "Why not?"

"Because you're wearing the irresistible expression of a woman who's just been thoroughly—" He broke off. "Trust me. One look at you and the hounds will be at your heels. Leave first and I'll catch up with you."

Feeling off-kilter, she stepped into her sandals and took a few deep breaths. She glanced back at him.

"I'll catch up in just a minute," he said.

She peeked out of the curtain and, seeing no one, she walked outside. The tropical breeze played over her skin, soothing her as she walked on the concrete next to the pool. What had she just done? she asked herself. Although Emma's sexual history was rather sparse, she couldn't recall any experience that had exploded with such passion. Physically, it had been unbelievable, but there'd been something deeper going on between them…unless she'd imagined it. And should she dare go to his room? Was she out of her mind?

Seconds later, she felt him step to her side and slide his hand around her back. "Okay?"

"Yes," she said, but her hands were trembling.

He caught one of them and slid his strong hand over hers. "Liar."

"I'm working on it," she said defensively. "I don't have that much experience with this kind of thing."

"Sex?" he asked, as he guided her toward the elevators.

She didn't want to admit just how limited her experience was. "With my boss in a cabana. New for me."

He chuckled. "I'm glad I got you carried away."

She took in a deep breath and entered the elevator as the doors whooshed open. She closed her eyes, hating how vulnerable she felt.

"What is it?" he asked.

They were the only people in the elevator. "This is going to sound really crazy, but I don't want you to think I'm easy."

He gave a bark of laughter. "Easy? I felt like I was breaking into Fort Knox."

Her heart lifted and her lips twitched. She threw him a sideways glance. "Slight exaggeration."

He shook his head. "I would have taken you in the office, in my car, in the limo, at the charity event…"

His confession squeezed her heart. "Why me?"

"You have something," he said, his eyes darkening. "You have something I've never had before and I want it."

The elevator dinged as it reached the top floor

and he glanced at the doors as they opened. "But it's up to you. You have the key to my suite," he said and walked out of the elevator.

Emma followed him outside of the elevator and slowly walked to her room. Standing outside her door, she looked further down the hall to Damien's room. She'd thought he was heartless and cold, but he was hotter than a fire on the coldest, scariest night of her life.

She wondered what she had that Damien could possibly want so much. Her heart did a strange flip-flop. Did she have the nerve to go to his room? Did she have the nerve *not* to go to him?

Ten

Two hours later, after they'd made love again, they sat together on the balcony with a blanket wrapped around them and the stars shining down. Her body was silky and warm within his arms.

"Have you ever done this before?" Emma asked, then shook her head. "Don't answer."

The truth was Damien had never felt magic the way he did tonight. "I haven't done this before, sat on a balcony with a beautiful woman in the middle of the night."

"I wouldn't say beautiful," she said.

"I would," he said.

"That's the sex talking," she said.

But it wasn't. Damien had glimpsed Emma's

sweetness and not only was she beautiful on the outside, she was beautiful on the inside. She was so loyal. He craved receiving that loyalty for himself.

"A lot of stars up there. What kind of wishes would you make?"

"If I believed in making wishes?" she asked.

"Yeah, I know," he said. "I made too many when I was a kid."

"Blowing out candles on a birthday cake," she said.

"Shooting star," he said.

She nodded.

"What kind of wishes would you make?"

She took a deep breath and nuzzled against his chin. "I would wish that my mother would never gamble again. That she would never *want* to gamble again."

"That makes sense." He slid his hand over her silky hair. "Name something frivolous."

She gave a soft chuckle. "Oh, wow. That's tough."

"So much has been about survival."

"That's right. You know, don't you?"

He felt her looking at him. "Yeah, I do." He paused. "So tell me something frivolous."

"I'm guessing world peace isn't acceptable."

He laughed, hugging her against him. "Not frivolous."

"Okay," she said, closing her eyes. "This is hard."

"You can do it."

She sighed and smiled. "A new apartment with a Jacuzzi and a wonderful pool."

"Sounds good."

"Losing ten pounds," she added.

"Don't even think about it. You don't need to lose anything."

She looked at him in disbelief. "You could have models, women with perfect bodies."

"Yours is perfect," he said, sliding his hands over her soft skin. "Name something else."

She closed her eyes. "A vacation somewhere exotic."

"Keep going."

"A dog."

"You mentioned that before. So you need a dog nanny, too," he said.

"Oh, I think that's going a bit far. Your turn. Name some wishes."

"I don't have wishes. I set goals. I give myself targets and exceed them."

"Spoken like a true tycoon," she said. "Okay, let's go further back, back to the time when you believed that blowing out the candles on that birthday cake meant your wish would come true."

He shook his head, lifting his hand to rub his jaw. "That's so far back. I don't know if I can remember. The first few years the family was split up, I made wishes that we could get back together. Wishes that my father and brother hadn't died in that train accident. Wishes that we hadn't been too much for my mother to deal with after it happened."

"That had to have been horrible," she said.

"Yeah, kinda hard to find something frivolous when your entire world has blown apart," he said.

"But you eventually decided you wanted a Ferrari," she said, with just enough humor to lift him out of his gloom.

He chuckled. "Yeah, I did, but you can be damn sure I didn't count on getting it by blowing out candles on a birthday cake."

"No, but it proves you've had some wishes," she said.

"Okay, back in the day, I wished for a bike where the chain didn't fall off every half mile."

"Did you ever get one?"

"Hell no. By the time I could afford one, I didn't care that much. I waited a long time to buy my first car because I used public transportation. That first car was a piece of—" He broke off and laughed. "Let me put it this way. It was no dream machine. The roof liner hung down on my head, the color was silver, metal and rust, and it drank oil like an alcoholic drinks booze."

"How did you accomplish so much with no support at all?"

He shrugged. "I worked," he said. "All the time. When I wasn't working, I was in school. By the time I hit twenty-two, I had three sideline businesses— commercial coffee service, accounting for small businesses and microstorage—when I started working for a firm that helped companies streamline and downsize when necessary. I worked my way to the top of that firm and they offered me a VP position. I passed and started my own company. My three sideline ventures exploded, demand for my services shot through the roof. I still lived like a poor foster kid and invested my money. All of a sudden I had more money than I knew what to do with."

"What a story," she said. "Talk about self-made. Has it been a total blur?"

He nodded. "A lot of it. The first time I celebrated Christmas in a long time was two years ago on my brother's yacht. My brother from Atlanta came down for the day."

"How was that?" she asked.

"Pathetic," he said, shaking his head. "It might as well have been a funeral. Until we started drinking and playing pool."

She chuckled. "Sounds interesting. Who won the game?"

"I did, of course. The two of them got way too sloshed. Rafe is always trying to do a rematch. I beat him almost every time."

Emma sighed and sat silently.

"What are you thinking?"

"I'm thinking at least you made a start at getting your family back together," she said. "And at least you have each other. That's more than a lot of people have. Nobody has a perfect life."

"Except for maybe Alex Megalos and Max De Luca," he said, his resentment rising suddenly.

"Neither of them has had a perfect life. Alex's father disowned him when he joined the company. And Max's father nearly ruined the company. On top of that, Max had to deal with his half brother. He was involved in criminal activity. Max's marriage didn't start out on the best foot, either." She stopped suddenly as if she realized she'd revealed far too much. "Of course, it's all better now and Max is a wonderful father."

Damien digested the information, filing each detail away for study at a later time. Emma may have just given him the key he needed to finish Max De Luca. He felt Emma give a little shiver. "Cold? I think it's time for me to take you back inside and warm you up."

Dressed in shorts and a tank top over her bikini, Emma accepted Damien's brother's hand as she boarded the yacht. She felt Damien just behind her.

"I'm Rafe. Welcome to my humble home at sea," he said and Emma saw the resemblance between brothers. Dark hair and dark eyes. At first glance, Rafe seemed to have a lighter air about him.

"Emma Weatherfield," she said. "I'm Damien's assistant at Megalos-De Luca. Thank you for inviting us."

She turned her attention to the large gleaming boat. Thankful that her expression was hidden by her sunglasses, Emma tried not to gawk.

Damien gave a rough chuckle. "Humble home? You wouldn't know humble if it jumped up and bit you."

"Nice to see you, too," Rafe said, shaking his brother's hand.

"It's generous of you to invite us on such short notice."

"It's not as if I had a choice. My brother is a dictator at heart. But it's my pleasure. If you should decide you'd like a change in environment, I'm certain I could use a woman with your talents in my organization."

"Don't start, Rafe," Damien said in a low voice with inlaid steel.

"I'm much more fun than he is," Rafe grumbled. "Let me show you around."

Rafe instructed one of the staff to get their drinks, then led them on a tour of the yacht, the upper level, below deck which included bedrooms, a well-equipped kitchen, an elegant but comfortable living area with a large-screen TV, and last, but not least, a game room with a pool table.

"I'm always trying to get your boss to come down and take some time off, shoot some pool, but he's married to the job," Rafe said.

"He just can't stand it that I beat him last time," Damien said.

"You're afraid of a rematch," Rafe goaded him.

"You always did have a vivid imagination," Damien said.

Rafe laughed. "Come on. Let's take this lady for a ride."

Out to sea they went. Damien made sure Emma sat in a perfect chair so she could enjoy the sun sparkling on the turquoise waters. A waiter or staff member, she wasn't sure which, made sure she was never without a drink. Damien sat with her for a while, then excused himself to chat with Rafe.

Suffering from a lack of sleep from her previous active night, Emma dozed. When she woke up, she immediately looked for Damien, but he wasn't close by. Rising from her lounge chair, she went in search of Damien and overheard him talking with his brother.

"How did you wind up with an assistant who looks like that?" Rafe asked.

"I don't know. Maybe De Luca was hoping to distract me."

"The man obviously doesn't know you," Rafe said.

"She's different," Damien admitted.

"I haven't heard you say that about a woman before," Rafe said.

"It doesn't matter," Damien said. "Her first loyalty is to MD."

"And her loyalty should be to you instead?" Rafe asked. "When you're not paying her salary and her entire future is tied up with MD."

"When you put it that way…"

"Yeah?"

"When you put it that way, it seems difficult for her to possibly choose to be loyal to me."

"Do you think De Luca has any idea who you are?" Rafe asked.

"He's too busy covering his own interests to see me as anything other than the person who is taking some control of his company away from him."

Emma's mind whirled from the exchange between the brothers. So Damien *knew* she was loyal to Max.

Yet, he'd made love to her. He'd held her on the balcony and she still thought he may have somehow been behind that Tesla Roadster. Yet, he'd been determined that she didn't know it was him. Confusion twisted through her. Why?

Damien glanced up and caught her gaze. "Emma, too much sun? Or did you get bored?"

She hesitated a second, unable to read his expression hidden by his dark sunglasses. "It's too beautiful to be bored."

"No seasickness?" Rafe asked.

She shook her head.

He smiled and the sun glinted on his wavy hair and white teeth, making him look like a movie star. She wasn't affected in the least.

"Good sailor. Good sign," he said.

"In what way?" she asked.

"A woman who can handle rough waters is a keeper," he said. "Are you sure I can't talk you into working for me?"

"Rafe," Damien said in a warning tone.

Rafe lifted his hands. "Can't blame a guy for trying."

"Once," Damien said. "That makes twice. More than enough."

"Cranky SOB," Rafe muttered and headed down below.

"You're a little hard on him," Emma said.

Damien slid his arm around her back and led her to the railing. "Rafe is one of those people that pushes as far as you let him."

"Even as a kid?" she asked, enjoying the warmth and weight of his arm around her.

"Even as a kid," he said, a smile playing on his lips. "He told wild stories to get out of trouble. He was the charmer, so he did okay with his foster parents. He only went through two before they stuck with him. They weren't wealthy, but they helped him through college. He wheeled and dealed and got into this business. Not too shabby," he said.

"No. He likes having you around, though, doesn't he?"

Damien nodded. "Yeah. For all his charm, he feels things more deeply than you'd expect. When my father died and my mother put us up for foster care, we were all just a little too old to blend in. We couldn't help wanting to go back."

"What about your brother in Georgia?"

"He's an overachiever, too," Damien said. "He feels guilty because he was the one who was supposed to have been riding that train with my dad. Survivor's guilt. Sucks. He drowns it in work."

"I see a common thread," she said.

Damien shot her a sideways glance. "I'm taking time off," he said. "I'm here, not doing the report, not doing assessments, with you."

His gaze shook her down to her bones. "Rough assignment, isn't it?"

His mouth slid into a sexy grin and he cupped her jaw, drawing her toward him. He slid his mouth over hers in a kiss that made her feel far dizzier than the motion of the ocean ever had. "When did you get to be so ornery?"

Good question, she thought, as she felt her knees turn to water and her mind to mud.

Emma gave into temptation and shared the rest of the time in South Beach with Damien in his suite. Every minute seemed to sparkle, so how could she possibly have any complaints about the resort?

She reviewed the resort with Damien on the return flight. "I'm trying to find something to criticize," she said. "Was it just me or was everything perfect?"

He met her gaze. "We're expected to prepare a report despite the fact that someone was obviously told that we were coming."

Emma felt a sliver of guilt. "Were the beds too soft? Too hard?"

"You sound like Goldilocks," he said with a chuckle.

"Okay, the food," she said. "What was wrong with the food?"

"Nothing," he said. "Breakfast was served promptly. Food was hot and prepared to order."

"Beach service?" she asked.

"Fine. Not too intrusive," he said, his gaze falling over her and making her warm.

Emma cleared her throat. "So, our recommendation is to buy."

He shook his head. "Our report is that the resort is extremely well-run under current management."

"Any recommendations?" she asked.

"Unfortunately, since the staff was obviously alerted to our presence, I can't offer any. Can you?"

Emma felt another stab of guilt at his question. "I guess you're right."

"I usually am," he said in a low voice that was far more resigned than cynical.

After they returned to the office, Emma struggled with her feelings for Damien. Behind their locked and closed doors, it was easy for him to come up beside her and stroke her hair. Sometimes he would call her into his office and would simply kiss her. This morning a dozen blush roses mixed with blue forget-me-not flowers arrived for her. No card, but she knew he'd sent them.

"Let me take you to dinner tonight. You've worked hard. I'd like to reward you. I need another hour to wrap things up. Does that work for you?"

The way he looked at her made her heart skip over itself. "I'm not sure it's a good idea for us to be seen in public. We don't want to give people the wrong idea," she said.

"Tell me. What's the wrong idea?" he asked, lifting her hand and sliding his mouth over the inside of her wrist.

It was all she could do not to press herself against him. "What's happened between us," she said.

"Happening," he corrected. "It's not over."

"It's temporary," she said. "I'll be here after you leave."

"And you don't want people to know you've been

fraternizing with the hatchet man," he said, his gaze never leaving her face.

She pulled her hand away. "If you're asking if I'm concerned about my reputation, the answer is yes. Like I said, you won't be staying. I will."

"I could offer you another option," he said.

"What?"

"You could come to work for me. I take care of my people. Ask my employees."

"The same way you've taken care of me?" she asked.

His jaw hardened. "No. I already told you there's something between you and me neither of us wants to pass up. I don't know why you continue to fight our relationship."

"It's just so complicated."

"It doesn't need to be. I want you, and I believe you want me."

She couldn't deny it, but she said nothing.

"I'm ordering dinner for two from Allister's and having it delivered to the office."

She gasped. Allister's was one of the finest restaurants in town. "That's ridiculous. Delivery alone will cost the earth."

"Hope you like champagne," he said with an infuriating hint of a grin just before he entered his office and closed the door behind him.

Eleven

Emma's moan of satisfaction immediately made him hard. Even though the source of her pleasure at the moment was chocolate hazelnut mousse, he could easily recall hearing that same sound when they'd shared his bed. Taking a sip of Dom Pérignon, he watched from below the rim of his flute. The more time he spent with her, the more he wanted from her. He wanted more than her sexual acquiescence; he wanted her affection, her trust, her loyalty. The strength of his desire surprised him.

"Hated the dessert, did you?" he asked, in a mock-serious tone.

She tossed him an accusing look. "How could I possibly turn down a meal from Allister's? With that mousse." She sighed. "I heard all kinds of terrifying things about your reputation, but nothing about how—" She broke off, frowning.

"About how?" he prompted.

"About how seductive you could be."

"That's because this is my first time at seduction. I don't have a lot of practice," he said, but she knew better.

"Right," she said in disbelief. "You clearly have no experience."

"Well," he said, pouring the last of the champagne into her glass. "The truth is I've never seduced a coworker. Too messy. But something about you…"

Her heart turned over. "You flatter me."

"No," he said and clicked his flute of champagne against hers. "I'm just telling the truth. So are you going to put me out of my misery and come over here and kiss me?"

Emma felt a rush of heat. "You don't look at all miserable."

"But I am," he said. "And you can save me from it."

It was such a ridiculous notion that she could save such a powerful man as Damien from anything. But his tie was askew and his gaze said *I want you.* He always invited, and she found his invitations completely irresistible.

Rising from her chair, she went to him and bent over, pressing her mouth against his. He pulled her into his lap and she couldn't muster a protest.

His arms felt wonderful. His mouth made her

forget the rest of the world. She could almost believe that she meant something special to him. Almost…

He took his time kissing her, exploring her mouth, making her feel taken and powerful at the same time. How could that be?

Her temperature rose and she wanted more. She tugged at the buttons of his shirt and pulled at his tie. He made her blouse dissolve and soon enough her breasts were bare. He pulled her over his hard masculinity and thrust inside her.

Emma gasped. He groaned in pleasure and began to coach her to rise and fall in a rhythm that made her sweat with need. Straddling him, she felt her nether regions clench around him.

Sliding his fingers through her hair, he brought her lips to his as he thrust inside her. Her climax began in fits and starts. She didn't think she could stand the sensations, but he kept on thrusting and she flew over the top. Seconds later, he followed, clenching her bottom, taking her mouth at the same time he took the rest of her, mind, body and, heaven help her, soul.

Breaths, minutes, centuries later, he held her against his chest, his heart beating against hers. "You leave first," he whispered. "I don't want people to gossip about you. If we leave together, they will. I'll follow you back to your apartment to make sure you arrive safely."

Still caught in the otherworld of their passion, Emma struggled to absorb his words. "Leave?" she echoed, lifting her head to meet his gaze.

He rubbed his finger over her lips and swore. "I want you again."

What Emma wanted was to stay in his arms all night. Longer if possible. She took a deep breath to gather her wits. "Leave," she said again.

"You first," he said. "I'll follow."

Reluctantly, she stood, separating herself from him. Her knees dipped in protest, but he caught her. "Okay?" he asked.

"Getting there," she said, but her mind was still muddy from passion. She grabbed her clothes and pulled them on. He did the same.

He looked into her eyes. "Do you need me to drive you home?"

She shook her head. "I'll be okay."

He paused a long moment. "I would rather you come back to my condo," he said.

She shook her head again. "Not a good idea."

He pulled her to him and took her mouth in a long, possessive kiss that rocked her world. Pulling away, he rubbed his thumb over her bottom lip. "You look like you've been thoroughly kissed."

She licked her lips, her tongue glancing his finger.

He swore under his breath.

"I have been thoroughly kissed," she whispered. "I should go."

He swore again.

"G'night."

Damien watched her leave, feeling a craving that went far beyond his groin, down to his bones. He couldn't remember wanting a woman this much. He'd thought the weekend in South Beach would ease his ache, but it had only made it worse. He wanted her and was determined to have her.

As she walked out of Megalos-De Luca headquarters, Emma felt like a sexual goddess. And a tramp. This was insane, she thought as she got into her Tesla Roadster and started the engine. It couldn't continue.

She took a deep breath and checked her rearview mirror, catching sight of her disheveled hair and swollen mouth. She had that just-got-out-of-bed look. Covering her eyes for a few seconds, she tried to gather her wits. She had gone totally over the edge with Damien.

Taking a deep breath, she pushed on the accelerator and drove out of the parking lot. Emma had kept herself in check for years. It had been a necessity with her mother's difficulties, but something about Damien had tempted her enough to let down her guard. Now, she needed to put it back in place. After all, she was technically supposed to be spying on Damien for work, not spying on him naked.

Glancing in her rearview mirror, she saw Damien's Ferrari. She needed to get control of this situation. Tomorrow, she told herself. Tomorrow would be the day.

The next morning, Damien arrived early, leaving a fresh bouquet of cream roses and forget-me-not flowers on Emma's desktop. Emma was turning into a constant craving, and he needed to do something about it. He decided she should move in with him. He would hire her away from MD with a higher salary and keep her. Until he got her out of his system. When would that be?

Although he could tell she was inexperienced, he found her completely irresistible. Hearing the door open, he felt his gut knot at her presence. In a matter of seconds, he would see her, hold her, kiss her.

Her footsteps slowed outside his office door. "Damien?" she said.

"Come in," he said, meeting her gaze.

She looked away. He noticed she wore a black dress and her face was pale with pronounced shadows under her eyes. She bit her lip.

His gut knotted again, this time in displeasure.

Taking a deep breath, she finally met his gaze. "I can't keep doing this," she said. "I'm just not cut out for an office affair. From now on, I have to keep our relationship strictly professional," she said, her voice breaking. "Being involved with you personally is too overwhelming. I can't think straight. I'm just not sophisticated enough to maintain this kind of affair."

The pain in her eyes kept him from sinking into a vat of bitterness. She was afraid, and perhaps rightly so, of the passion that flared between them. She wanted a measure of safety, and to her, he represented a total free fall.

He couldn't help, however, feeling disappointed.

He knew she felt the same way he did. He knew he could make her take back those words right now if he wanted. Her vulnerability stopped him.

He had wanted her to choose him. He wanted her to open herself to him in every possible way. At the same time, he kept himself protected.

"I understand," he finally said, but was determined that he would change her mind.

Twenty-four hours later, a call came in, chilling Emma to the bone. The voice mail had come through when she'd been in a meeting, taking notes for Damien.

"Sweetie," her mother said, her voice breaking. "I'm so sorry, but I've gotten into trouble again."

Within an hour, Emma learned her mother had latched on to Internet gambling and had lost a quarter of a million dollars. Emma was reeling.

The next day she went to work and tried to hide it, but her fear must have shown through her usual calm.

"What's going on?" Damien asked.

"It's personal," she said, unable to meet his gaze.

He wheeled her chair around so that she was facing him and put his hands on the armrests. "You and I have gotten about as personal as a man and woman can get. Tell me what has upset you."

Her stomach clenched and she bit her lip. She felt so ashamed and desperate. Even though she hadn't been the one to gamble, she somehow felt responsible. "I need to sell the roadster."

"Why?" he asked.

"Because I need the money," she whispered.

"For what?"

She still couldn't meet his gaze. "I just have to do it. Can you help me?"

He paused a beat. "Yes. What do you need?"

"A quarter of a million dollars," she said, her throat constricting into a painful knot.

"What the hell would you need—" He broke off. "Your mother," he said.

His correct guess immediately made her feel as if at least half a ton had been lifted from her shoulders. She took a deep breath and exhaled.

"How in the world did she get into gambling again? Didn't you say she'd left Vegas?"

"Online gambling," Emma told him and finally met his gaze. He saw a mixture of confusion and concern.

"Damn," he said, raking his fingers through his hair. "You know the problem with bailing her out is—"

"It could happen again," she said miserably. "But there's no way she could pay this off on her own. And I'm terrified of what those loan shark lenders would do to her. What if they hurt her? What if they—" She couldn't bring herself to say her worst fear.

"It's clear that your mother has an addiction," he said.

"Yes," she agreed.

"I think the best plan would be to pay off her debts and get her into an intense treatment."

"What do you mean?"

"I mean I think she needs to go to a specialized treatment facility and stay until she's truly strong enough to manage her addiction on an outpatient basis."

Emma's head spun at the prospect. "I don't even know if such a facility exists. She's not addicted to drugs."

"I'm sure it exists," Damien said. "We just need to find the most successful one."

"That sounds expensive," she said.

"The alternative isn't cheap," he pointed out.

She nodded in agreement. "I'm just not sure I can afford it."

"I can," he said.

Emma stared at Damien in amazement. "Pardon me?"

"I said I have enough money." Damien gave a wry laugh. "I have money to burn."

"But—"

"You and I can negotiate an arrangement."

Emma frowned, feeling an undercurrent of fear and doubt. "Arrangement?"

"Very simple," he said. "I pay off your mother's debts, you keep your Tesla. You remain my lover and faithful, loyal assistant."

Emma stared at him in disbelief. "You're suggesting that I trade my loyalty in exchange for you paying for my mother's mistakes?"

"I'll compensate you in other ways financially, of course. Seems a fair trade to me," he said.

Emma fought a wave of nausea. "So, I sell myself and my integrity for the sake of my mother."

"That's more harsh than it needs to be. You've been to bed with me. You know we can take care of each other."

Squeezing her forehead, she bit her lip as she thought of the implications. "I would have no future with MD."

"I would take care of you."

"Until you grew tired of me," she said, meeting his gaze. "How long do you propose for this to last?"

Silence swelled between them.

"Until you grow tired of me," she repeated, her stomach twisting violently.

"Actually, I would say indefinitely," he told her, leaning toward her. "I've never met a woman like you. A woman with your combination of qualities. I'm not sure I ever will again."

She saw something in his eyes, want, need, that made his offer feel just a little more palatable. Yet… "I need to think about this," she said.

"How much time do you have?"

"Not much with the people she owes," Emma said. "The problem with bailing her out is that it doesn't give her an opportunity to face her illness."

He nodded. "That's why she may need more than bailout money. Money for treatment. Think about it and let me know."

Emma barely slept at all that night. She tossed and turned. How could she possibly sell her loyalty? Her integrity? The possibility sickened her. She struggled to find an alternative, any alternative, but all the possibilities left her in debt for the rest of her life with the chance that her mother would fall again.

Emma knew that her mother needed to face her creditors for herself and that a bailout was not going to help her mother take responsibility for herself. She just couldn't imagine any other solution. Her mother would never make enough money to pay off her debt. What if her so-called creditors got rough with her? What if they killed her?

Emma wouldn't be able to live with herself if she allowed that to happen. Her mother clearly needed intensive treatment, expensive treatment.

After an endless night, morning finally arrived and Emma applied blush and extra concealer to hide her stress and the dark circles under her eyes. Wearing a cream-colored business dress, she walked into the office, wishing she were wearing sunglasses. A little extra armor would be great. Damien was already in his office. No surprise there. She tapped on his door.

"Yes?" he said.

"It's Emma."

"Come in," he said.

She walked inside, but didn't take a seat. He rose, which forced her to look up to him.

"Good morning," he said.

"The jury's still out on that," she said. "You've made me an offer. I'd like to nail down the terms."

"I thought I made it clear. I'll pay for your

mother's treatment and her debts in exchange for your loyalty as my assistant and my lover."

"I'd like an expiration date on that," she said.

He lifted his eyebrows in surprise. "Really?"

"Really," she said.

"Okay. Two years," he said.

"One," she countered.

He paused. "Okay, but we both may want to re-negotiate."

"I just want the ground rules," she said. "I'll need to take a couple days off."

"Fine. I'll transfer the funds to whatever account you want."

Emma felt another ball of nausea rise to her throat, but she took a deep breath to counter the terrible sensation. This was the best way out of a bad situation. She pulled out a deposit slip from her bank account and gave it to him. "Thank you," she said in a low voice.

"Emma," he said and she felt too much just from the way he said her name.

Shaking her head, she tried to get her emotions in check. "I have a lot of things to do. I'll talk to you later," she said and left his office.

She immediately took the elevator to the executive offices. Hearing the echo of her heels clicking down the hallway, she headed for Alex's office first. She'd always felt Alex was a little more human than Max. It would be easier to tell Alex than Max. Unfortunately, according to his assistant, Alex wouldn't be in today.

Gathering her courage, she walked to Max's office. He, of course, was there, and immediately welcomed her.

"Good to see you, Emma. You're doing a great job," he said, motioning toward a chair in his office suite. "Great warning on the South Beach site. I think we were able to head off any objections from the board."

"I can't do this anymore," she said, remaining standing.

He stared at her for a moment. "Excuse me?"

"I can no longer be a spy against Damien Medici. It's too hard for me to try to be helpful to him at the same time that I'm supposed to be working against him." Sensing Max's extreme disappointment and disapproval, she felt her stomach twist and turn. "I'm sorry, but I just can't do it. I understand if you want to release me."

Silence sat in the room like a heavy, undigested meal. "No," he said. "What we asked you to do would be difficult for most, impossible for many. Damien won't be here forever. You've been a loyal employee. You'll always have a job at Megalos-De Luca Enterprises as long as I have a say."

"Thank you," she said, feeling like a traitor. "That means a lot."

Still sick with worry over her mother, Emma left headquarters and went to her apartment. The familiarity of her surroundings provided little comfort with her personal and professional life in such upheaval. Pulling out her laptop, she began to research the success rate of facilities designed to help people with gambling addictions. Within days, her mother's debts would be paid, but the larger problem of her mother's illness had to be addressed.

Later that evening as she ate a sandwich and checked flights going to Missouri, a knock sounded at her door. Emma rose and checked the peephole, surprised to see Damien, still dressed in the suit he'd been wearing that morning, on her doorstep. Struggling with an odd sense of combined relief and dread, she opened the door. "Hi."

"Hi," he said in return. "I thought I should check on you to see what your plans are."

"Come in," she said. "I was just looking at flights to Missouri. I've been doing some research on residential treatment facilities."

"I asked my company assistant to do some research, too," he said and pulled an envelope from his coat pocket. "Here's a list of three that are reputable and have high success rates."

Surprised at his thoughtfulness, she accepted the envelope. "Thank you."

"You're welcome. There's no need to fly commercial. You can use my company jet."

Emma shook her head. "That's not necessary. I wouldn't feel right about it."

"I said I would take care of you," he reminded her. "You don't need to do this alone. I can come with you."

Emma bit her lip and fought the strange urge to lean on his strength. She had no doubt that Damien could take care of her. Heaven help her, this situation was complicated. The problem with letting him take care of her was that she dare not get used to it.

"No. It's best if I handle this myself. You're already contributing too much financially," she said.

"Emma, you haven't made a deal with the devil," he told her. "Look at me. You can count on me."

Twelve

Emma made the tough trip to Missouri and confronted her mother about her gambling addiction. She called it that: an addiction. Her mother cried, but confessed her weakness and her need.

Emma required her mother to personally pay off her creditors. Then her mother agreed that she needed help. Emma proposed on-site treatment and to her surprise, her mother leaped at the opportunity. She helped her mother pack and joined her on a flight to the treatment facility she hoped would get her mother on the right track.

Seventy-two hours after she'd first left Las Vegas, her return flight touched down on the runway back home. She was so exhausted she could cry, but she still needed to grab a cab and go home.

She pulled her carry-on bag through the airport, past the slot machines that lured arrival passengers to take a chance and win. The big jackpot was only one pull of the handle away. The thought made her stomach turn. The elusive promise of winning big had continually seduced her mother and made her home life unstable.

Emma didn't believe in the big payoff. In fact, she feared the promise of it, because it never lasted. She walked outside the terminal to catch a cab. Instead of a taxi, however, a low-slung Ferrari pulled alongside the curb and stopped.

Her heart took a dip. It couldn't possibly be Damien. She hadn't been in touch with him since she'd left.

But there he was, stepping out of the driver's side of the car and taking her bag to put it in the trunk. Too weary to be anything but grateful, Emma slid inside the passenger seat and practically melted into the leather.

"How'd it go?" he asked, pulling forward.

"As well as could be expected," she said, leaning back against the headrest. "My mother admitted she has a huge problem and wanted help. All I had to do was mention a treatment facility and she jumped at the opportunity."

"Good. She's lucky to have you as her daughter," he said.

Emma closed her eyes. "It's crazy, but when I was little, I always wondered if she had this problem because of me. Maybe if I hadn't been born or if I was different or—"

"None of that," Damien said with a hint of ruthlessness in his voice. "You're the best thing your mother has. I bet she would say the same thing."

Emma took a deep breath at the same time her heart fluttered. She didn't want to be under Damien's spell. She wanted, no needed, to be in control. "Thank you for picking me up at the airport."

"You're welcome," he said. "Do you need anything to eat?"

Emma shook her head at the same time her stomach growled. "Kids' meal takeout would be great."

"Can do," he said and within minutes placed an order at a drive-thru window.

Emma opened her eyes when Damien paid. The fast food server gawked at the Ferrari.

She smiled. "I guess he doesn't see these every day."

"Guess not," Damien said, sliding a sideways glance at her as she dug into a kids' meal cheeseburger with mustard and pickles. "How is it?"

"Not quite the level of Allister's, but ambrosia at the moment," she said.

"I'm taking you back to my condo tonight. Your place is further from the airport and since tomorrow is Sunday, I thought you could sleep in."

Too weary to argue, she moved her head in a circle. "I'm sure I'll fall asleep the second my head hits the pillow."

In fact, Emma must have fallen asleep as soon as

she finished her burger and a few fries. She awakened to being carried in Damien's arms inside a dimly lit room where she'd never been.

Shaking her head, she glanced around. "What—"

"Shh, you'll wake up the baby," he said.

Emma blinked. *Baby?* Then she realized Damien was referring to her. She couldn't swallow a soft laugh. "Already done. The baby's awake and wants to brush her teeth and wash her face before she goes into a coma again."

He allowed her to slide down his body until her feet touched the floor. "Master bath is to the right. My housekeeper keeps a basket of toiletries underneath the sink."

After a stressful trip and a day of harsh travel, Damien's voice soothed her nerves and his strength felt like a warm blanket. "Thank you for bringing me upstairs."

"No problem," he said. "Do you want a bath?"

"That sounds wonderful," she said. "Tomorrow." Emma padded into the luxurious bathroom and quickly washed her face and brushed her teeth. Realizing she needed her gown, she remembered it was in her bag. She returned to the bedroom. "My ba—" She broke off when she saw Damien standing in nothing but lounge pants. His gleaming broad shoulders and bare chest captured her attention.

"You needed something?" he prompted.

Despite the fact that she should be too tired to keep her eyes open let alone gawk at Damien's body, she couldn't fight a ripple of awareness that ran throughout her body. She cleared her throat. "My bag. I need my gown."

He nodded toward the side of the room where she stood. "There."

She glanced in the same direction he had, sheepish that the bag had been positioned right beside her. Pulling her gown from her carry-on, she scooted back into the bathroom and put it on. Moments later, she returned to find Damien already in bed with the covers folded back.

Feeling a strange twist of nerves, she climbed into bed, hugging the opposite side. Three heartbeats later, she felt his hand wrap around her belly, and he pulled her back against the front of him. "Relax," he said in a low voice against her ear. "Go to sleep."

Seconds later, she did.

The next morning she awakened to the delicious sensation of being in his arms. He nuzzled the back of her neck and she held her breath in anticipation of him making love to her. Instead, he got out of bed. "Be lazy," he instructed her. "I'll be reading the paper outside on the terrace."

Surprised that he hadn't taken sexual advantage of sharing a bed with her, she stared after him for a moment. Then she decided to follow orders and fell back asleep.

After a leisurely bath, she joined him and sunned

on the terrace wearing a pair of his shorts and a cut-off black T-shirt. They snacked on sandwiches prepared by his housekeeper. He touched her frequently, stroking her hair, sliding his hand over the bare skin of her torso.

The intermittent contact put her in a state of perpetual awareness. She felt as if a low hum of arousal buzzed inside her. He almost made her forget that they had made a deal, and she had practically sold herself to him.

He surprised her by preparing dinner. "All the Medici men cook. My father taught us at a young age. His father taught him and so on."

Emma watched him as he prepared a sauce with plum tomatoes, spinach, olive oil, spices. "That smells delicious."

"It will be," he said.

"Did your father ever live in Italy? Or was he raised here?"

Damien's jaw tightened. "He moved to the States when he was seventeen. His family went through a rough time in Italy and his father lost the family home in a business deal where he was cheated. Pretty much ruined them."

"That's terrible," she said.

He nodded. "Yeah. Things were looking up for my father right before he died, and everything fell apart again."

"You miss him," she said, sensing his grief.

"Yes. It was ironic. He and his brothers and sisters

were torn apart and the same thing happened to my brothers and me."

"I bet he would be proud of how well you've done," she said.

"Maybe," he said. "He was from the old school where if someone hurt a member of your family, it was your duty to pay them back."

"He wasn't Mafia, was he?" she asked, his dark tone making her wary.

Damien laughed. "No. Just very Italian. Here, try the sauce." He lifted a spoonful and blew on it before he extended it to her lips.

Emma tasted the spicy sauce and nodded. "Delicious."

"Yes, you are," he said, intently meeting her gaze.

They shared dinner on the terrace. Afterward, he coaxed her into taking a nude dip with him in the Jacuzzi surrounded by a teak lattice privacy screen. She'd thought all her tension from the trip was gone, but the velvet darkness and hot massaging water relaxed her even more.

"This is wonderful. It's a good thing I don't have one of these. I'd never get out," she said, feeling decadent and languid as she sipped the champagne he'd poured for her. "How often do you use it?"

"A couple of times since I arrived," he said, watching her from beneath a hooded gaze as he slid one of his legs between hers. "I've been too busy."

She felt another rush of arousal ooze through her.

She watched his gaze linger on her lips. Taking her hand, he lifted it to his mouth.

He was suddenly too far away and she suddenly couldn't wait a minute longer to be close to him. She moved closer and he immediately pulled her onto his lap. Skimming his hands over her naked, wet body underwater, he lowered his head and took her mouth in a sensual kiss that made her breathless.

He touched the tips of her breasts and kissed her again. "I've been thinking," he said.

"Oh, no," she said, her brain muddled by his effect on her.

"It's not so bad. I've been thinking that you and I should make our arrangement permanent."

Confusion warred with arousal. She frowned. "Permanent," she echoed.

He played with her nipples again, short-circuiting her thought process. "I think we should get married."

Shock raced through her and she gawked at him. "Married? I—I—"

He shot her a half grin before he took her mouth again, his hands distracting her. "Think it over," he murmured against her mouth. "Later."

Awakening the next morning to the sound of Damien in the shower, Emma stretched, feeling the aftereffects of Damien's repeated lovemaking. She covered her face with the sheet when she thought of how uninhibited she'd been.

Shaking off her self-consciousness, she rose from

his bed and pulled on the nightgown she'd never worn last night and went into the kitchen to make coffee. The scent of fresh coffee in a timed maker told her she was too late for that.

She poured herself a cup and added sugar and milk, then gingerly sipped the hot liquid. Hearing the scream of a fax machine, she walked down the hallway and opened the door to an office. A large cherry desk dominated the room lit by three-quarter length windows covered with linen shades.

The fax machine continued to scream and she heard a rustle of paper. Emma rearranged the paper in case it was jammed. Seconds later, several sheets flew onto the floor. Although she wasn't trying to read the fax, her gaze snagged on the name Max De Luca. Quickly scanning the document, she gleaned that it was a report with references to Max's late half brother.

Damien appeared in the doorway, already dressed in black slacks, his shirt not yet buttoned. He lifted a dark eyebrow of inquiry.

"I heard a strange noise from the fax machine. It sounded jammed, so I tried to clear it. What is this about Max De Luca?"

Damien walked toward her and she handed him the papers. "It's a report. I had him investigated. It's not unusual."

"But this mentions his brother. Well, the brother that died. Tony," she said, still confused.

Damien read over the paper. "It appears that Tony briefly worked for MD and stole some money from the company. One of the company attorneys was determined to prosecute. This says Max De Luca not only paid Tony's debt, he also paid the attorney to keep quiet and accept a transfer. Wonder what the board would think of this."

Emma gasped. "You wouldn't tell them, would you? I can't imagine why you would. It doesn't have anything to do with the downsizing."

Damien's jaw tightened. "Always protective of Max and Alex," he said in a velvet voice with an undertone of bitterness. "Don't worry. This is between Max and me."

Confused, she shook her head. "I don't understand."

He thumped the paper with his forefinger. "No. You wouldn't. You remember the story I told you about how my grandfather lost the family home in a business deal where he was cheated?"

"Yes," she said, wondering where this was going.

"Max De Luca's grandfather was the man who cheated my grandfather. My family home is a Megalos-De Luca resort."

"Oh, no," she said, horrified by the connection. Her mind and heart racing, she reached out to him. "That's horrible." She could hardly believe it. "I can't believe Max knows about this. He truly is an honorable man."

"Some might not agree," Damien said, tapping the papers that gave damning evidence.

Her stomach tightened in apprehension. "But you wouldn't use that against him because of something his grandfather did." A long moment of silence passed and she felt a terrible sense of dread. "Would you?"

"Three generations of my family have suffered in some part due to what the De Lucas did to my grandfather," he told her.

His harsh expression made her feel as if she were looking at a different man than the Damien she'd come to know. "How long have you known this?" she asked, trying to make sense of it all. "Why did you accept this assignment if you hated him so—" She broke off, suddenly realizing that Damien had taken the job with revenge in mind.

Emma felt as if her world had been turned upside down. If Damien was so consumed with revenge, where did she fit into the plot? He'd known she was protective of Max and Alex. He'd known…

Realization broke through. Her mind flashed back to that time when she'd told Damien about Max's and Alex's vulnerabilities. He'd used that information to dig deeper into Max's situation with his half brother. She'd given him the clue and he'd run with it.

Nausea swept through her. "You were just using me."

"Just as you were using me. Do you think I didn't know that you went to Alex and Max every time I told you something important?"

Humiliation stung. Overwhelmed, she shook her head. "I was doing my job."

"You tried to spy on me," he said.

The truth hurt, but her heart hurt even more. "I almost thought you cared about me."

"The irony is that I do, and I know you care about me. The situation is unfortunate."

"And you mentioned marriage last night. How could you even begin to think we could have a successful marriage?"

"You thought we could, too," he said. "Admit it."

Never, she thought. "I would never marry you, because I'd only marry for love, and you're not capable of it."

Thirteen

Damien tried to reason with Emma, but she recoiled at his touch. Concerned for her emotional state, he insisted on calling his driver to take her home. She left his condo without a backward glance.

The way she'd looked at him, as if he were a monster, sliced at his gut, but he pushed it aside. He had what he needed to bring down Max De Luca. For the sake of his family, he couldn't stop now.

Damien decided, however, that he wanted an opportunity to talk with Max before he took his final action. Giving his assistant a call, he was immediately put through to Max, and the VP agreed to meet with him.

He carried the report sealed in an envelope in his inner jacket pocket. In a way, he may as well have been carrying a loaded weapon. Max's assistant informed him of Damien's presence and he was ushered inside the VP's richly appointed office.

"Good morning, Damien," Max said. "Sarah, can you get us some coffee please? How do you take yours?"

"Black," Damien said.

Max nodded. "Same. Please have a seat," he said, motioning toward the leather chairs and sofa on the opposite side of the room as the desk. The magnificent view from the floor-to-ceiling windows revealed the mountains in the distance.

"Nice view," Damien said. It occurred to Damien that Max had never spent a day of his life outside the lap of luxury, a life far different than that of his family.

"I prefer the mountains to the strip. More serene."

Sarah delivered the coffee and excused herself.

"I understand employees who are being laid off will receive the news tomorrow?" Max asked, taking a sip of his coffee. "I have to confess I was against you from the beginning. Your reputation precedes you. When I look at the new organizational chart, however, it looks as if you skillfully used a scalpel instead of a hatchet."

Surprised by the praise, he nodded. "There is a right way and a wrong way to reorganize. Sometimes it takes an objective eye to spot redundancies and stay current with changing economies and needs."

"It's a painful process, but I think you made it as humane as possible. So, what do you have going next?"

The conversation felt surreal. Damien was talking

to the man he'd targeted for most of his life. He worked to access his contempt for the man, but for some reason it wasn't as strong as before.

"I may take some time off. I have a brother in Florida who is always bugging me to visit him."

Max lifted his eyebrows. "Time off? You don't strike me as the type. I know I wasn't until I got married. Lilli changed my priorities. Hell," he said. "She changed my life."

"The love of a good woman," Damien said.

Max nodded. "Yeah, although I would have been the last man to believe it was possible. Being a father will turn you around, too."

Silence lingered for a moment. "I'm curious," Damien said. "Did you know your grandfather well?"

"No. I do know that he was very focused on the company. He was determined to expand the empire, so to speak. My father had his own issues. It was left to me to try to rebuild the De Luca name. I had a half brother, but that's another sad story. What makes you ask?"

"Are you familiar with the MD Chateau on the outside of Florence, Italy?" Damien watched Max's face carefully.

Max furrowed his brow in concentration. "It's not in the city? Right?"

"No. It's in the countryside."

"I have a vague recollection, but I don't think I've ever visited it." He lifted his hand and met Damien's gaze. "Why? Is there a problem with it?"

"More the way it was acquired," he said.

"Okay," Max replied, leaning forward, lacing his fingers together. "What do you know about it?"

"I know that Chateau Megalos-De Luca was once Chateau de Medici and it belonged to my grandfather."

Fifteen minutes later, Damien walked out of Max De Luca's office feeling much different than he had going in. He stepped into the elevator thinking that Max De Luca had actually been somewhat reasonable. The damning report about the man felt as if it were burning a hole in his coat pocket.

Damien had spent most of his life fighting one thing or another, the loss of his family, an abusive foster parent, and poverty. He'd always thought that taking down Max De Luca would rid him of one of his biggest demons at the same time it would help right the wrong done to his grandfather.

Now that he had the chance to do it, his appetite for revenge had fled. It wasn't that Max De Luca was Mr. Nice Guy, because he wasn't. During that conversation with Max, though, Damien had seen glimpses of himself in the man he'd been prepared to hate.

Max was a family man. His top priority was taking care of his family. That was why he'd protected his half brother. Max's growing-up situation didn't sound all that rosy, either. His eyes lit up when he mentioned his wife and baby.

Exiting the elevator, Damien couldn't squelch his envy at the man's personal happiness. He couldn't help thinking about Emma and how he felt when he was with her. Just her presence made the world seem better. It was odd as hell, but she made him want to be better.

Swearing under his breath, he walked into his private office and paced the length of it. He pulled the envelope out of his pocket and stared at it. This was the opportunity he'd been waiting for most of his life. He had the gun and the bullet. All he had to do was pull the trigger.

Five minutes later, he'd made his decision and his deed, as far as he was concerned, was done. Hearing the door to the office suite open, he glanced into the outer office, surprised to see Emma.

His heart stuttered in his chest. "I didn't expect you to come in," he said.

She met his gaze, her eyes colder than ice. "I made an agreement. I try very hard to keep my word."

She slid into her chair and turned on her computer. She clearly hated him. The knowledge stabbed at him. The pain he felt took him by surprise. How had she become so important to him? He'd thought he had everything under control.

"I've done some thinking about our agreement," he said.

She shot him a look of suspicion, but said nothing.

"I'm terminating it effective immediately."

Her eyes widened in surprise. "I don't know how long it will take me to pay you back that kind of money, but—"

He lifted his hand. "You fulfilled your part of the agreement. You owe me nothing."

"But—" She lifted her hand to her throat. "But you said a year."

"I changed my mind," he said, giving her a wry smile. "Billionaire's prerogative. I can't buy your loyalty or your trust. I'm not sure I would want to if I could." He shrugged. "I'm cleaning out my office. I've finished this project. You can take off the rest of the day. Except one thing," he said. "I'd like you to make sure the paper in the shredder basket is destroyed."

She looked at him in confusion. "Okay. Would you like me to do that now?"

"Yes, I would," he said and stepped aside so she could go into his office to collect the basket. He caught a draft of her subtle, sweet scent as she passed him and clenched his jaw. He would never hold her again.

"Where do you want me to take it?" she asked.

"Somewhere off-site," he said.

She dipped her head in surprise.

"It's the report on Max De Luca," he said.

Her jaw dropped and she looked at him in surprise, followed by hope, followed by confusion. Clearing her throat, she licked her lips and nodded. "I'll take care of it right away," she said softly.

"Thank you," he said, meeting her gaze for a long moment, his mind replaying the times she'd smiled at him, the times she'd come to him and kissed him, the time they'd talked about wishes, and she'd made him start wishing again.

She looked away. "Thank you," she finally said. "For everything."

"Goodbye," he said, more for himself than for her. She was never going to be his. Never.

Emma considered stopping to throw the shredded report away at a mall, a service station, a fast-food restaurant. None seemed right, so she drove all the way to her apartment.

She was in shock, numb. She'd been so furious earlier this morning when she'd realized he'd used her. Furious with him for pointing out her deception with him. She considered her so-called spying assignment with Damien to be the lowest thing she'd ever done.

Then when she'd learned he had information he planned to use against Max, information she'd helped him find, she hadn't known who she detested more, Damien or herself.

It had taken everything in her to show up for work. She had to stick to the agreement for her mother's sake. She was fully prepared to despise him and resent him for the rest of her life.

But then he'd let her off the hook. No reprisals, no you-owe-me, nothing. On top of that, telling her to destroy the remnants of the report about Max totally boggled her mind. She didn't know what to think or feel.

Parking her car in the paved parking lot, she walked inside her apartment to get some matches and a pitcher of water. She returned to the parking lot, dumped the contents of the bin onto the pavement and burned them. Staring into the fire, she wondered what had made Damien decide not to go after Max. She wondered what had changed his mind.

As Damien had instructed, she took off the rest of the day. She caught up on cleaning her apartment and doing laundry, turned on the television for a while, then turned it off. Fighting a bone-deep restlessness, she escaped her apartment and visited a park.

She saw a couple and thought of Damien. She saw a golden retriever and thought of Damien. Frustrated with herself, she went to a movie by herself, a foreign film, French. Surely that would distract her. Except midway through the movie, an Italian character was introduced. She began to feel haunted.

Bedtime finally arrived and Emma crawled into bed, craving escape from Damien. Instead, she dreamed of him. She dreamed he died and she woke up in a cold sweat, screaming.

Hugging her knees to her chest, she gasped for breath. Something had changed, she realized. Without really knowing it, some part of her had begun to count on him. She'd been so busy doubting him, but something inside her had made another determination about him.

Her heart? Somehow, someway, she had begun to love him.

Her stomach twisted with the realization and she laughed, the harsh, bitter sound breaking the silence of the night. How futile was that? she thought. If ever a man was incapable of love, it was Damien.

Damien missed his next shot. He was winning against his brother, but not by much.

Rafe downed a shot of tequila and made a hissing sound. "You're off your game, bro," he said and chalked the cue.

"I'm doing okay," Damien said, taking a sip of scotch.

"Got something on your mind?" Rafe asked, banking a shot that just missed the pocket. "Damn," he muttered and raked his hand through his hair. "What's up? You've been walking around crabby and distracted since you got here."

Damien shrugged. "This was a big contract. Sometimes it takes awhile to wind down." He took a shot against another ball. And missed. He swore under his breath.

"Sounds like BS to me," Rafe said. He took a shot and sank it into the pocket. "Score," he said, then missed the next one.

Damien gritted his teeth and lined up his next shot.

"This wouldn't have anything to do with that pretty assistant you brought onboard when you visited South Beach a few weeks ago, would it?"

Damien scratched the table with his cue and glared at his brother for his bad timing. "I wouldn't go there if I were you."

"Why not?" Rafe asked. "If I keep pushing on that

raw place, I may win. Then I can hold it over your head for years."

"In your dreams," Damien said.

Rafe chuckled but missed his next shot.

Damien swallowed a growl and chalked his cue.

"She must not have liked you. Did she dump you?" Rafe taunted.

Damien clenched his jaw, then forced himself to relax.

"Did she decide she wanted a man with a heart *and* brains?"

Rafe's words cut close, but Damien ruthlessly turned him off. He focused on his shot and sank the last ball into the pocket. Taking a deep breath, he heard Rafe swear and lifted his glass of scotch in salute.

"How do you do that? Even on an off day," Rafe said.

"I'm hungrier than you are," Damien said. He felt not an ounce of satisfaction at beating his brother. "I always have been."

"Hungry enough to go after Miss Emma Weatherfield?" Rafe asked.

Damien met Rafe's gaze. "I've been hungry to survive, to succeed. Women come and go. I'm usually glad when they go."

"But not this time," Rafe said with a knowing glance.

Damien sighed. "You can be a real pain in the butt."

Rafe stretched his lips in a sharklike smile. "Part of my charm." His brother moved toward him and clapped him on the back. "I think you've met your waterloo."

Damien shook his head, not wanting it to be true. But

it was. "She despises me. I—" He paused. "I seduced information out of her. She'll never forgive me."

"If she surrendered to the seduction, then she can't totally despise you," Rafe said.

Damien threw him a sideways glance.

"Unless you blew it in some other way."

Damien shifted from one foot to the other.

"Like omitting the four-letter word that starts with *L*," Rafe said.

"What makes you an expert?" Damien asked, feeling as if he was being fried alive.

Rafe lifted his hand. "Nothing. I've just heard that women really want to hear the L word. For some of them, it's a requirement. But if she's not a keeper, then—"

"She's a keeper," Damien retorted.

Silence followed and he met Rafe's gaze again.

Rafe lifted his eyebrows. "I think you just answered your question."

Damien sank into a leather chair and exhaled. "It's not that easy. I screwed it up."

"That hasn't stopped you from succeeding with your business or anything else you've wanted. Why would it stop you now?"

Damien raked his fingers through his hair. "You don't know."

"I don't have to," Rafe said. "I just know that if this woman makes you feel like you found home, then you better find a way to keep her or you'll spend the rest of your life regretting it."

* * *

Emma pulled her Tesla Roadster into a parking spot just outside her condominium and cut the engine. Sitting for a moment, she leaned against the steering wheel and stared out the window.

A familiar restlessness rippled through her. Maybe it was time for her to leave Las Vegas. Maybe it was time for her to leave Megalos-De Luca.

The mere notion was shocking. She'd thought she would stay at MD forever, but lately she'd felt dissatisfied and unhappy. She felt like Goldilocks, except there was no "just right."

Sighing, she dismissed her ongoing dissatisfaction and rose from her car. She had a great job with excellent pay, a fabulous car and nice friends. She had no reason to whine.

Since Damien had completed his contract with MD, she'd been reassigned to a new VP, a nice older gentleman planning to retire in two years. Her stomach no longer knotted in apprehension as she arrived at the headquarters. Her heart didn't race. Everything was back to normal.

Emma had never thought she'd want anything but a normal, stable life until now. She missed Damien. She missed his passion. She missed his strength. She even missed his flaws.

"You can't have him," she whispered to herself. "So stop thinking about him."

Stepping inside her apartment, she closed the door behind her. She heard a scratching sound and— A bark? Seconds later, a small mass of fur with long floppy ears ran toward her barking and wagging its tail.

Emma gaped at the puppy and immediately kneeled to the floor. "Who are you? And how did you get in here?"

The white-and-caramel colored spaniel jumped into her lap. How had the dog gotten into her apartment? Emma laughed as the puppy licked her chin.

"Lucky dog," said a low, familiar voice from the doorway.

Emma's heart stuttered. She jerked her head upward and stared at Damien as he leaned against the doorjamb. She blinked to make sure she wasn't hallucinating.

"What are you—" Her chest squeezed so tightly that she couldn't finish her question.

"Doing here?" he finished for her and pushed away from the doorjamb, walking toward her. "Some people would say I'm a glutton for punishment, but when I find something I want, I don't like to quit."

Emma bit the inside of her lip. "Something?" she said.

"Someone," he said and extended his hand.

She slid her hand in his strong, warm palm and allowed him to help her stand.

"You like your new dog?" he asked, his lips lifting in a faint smile as the puppy danced at their feet.

"Mine?" she echoed. "I work all day. I shouldn't

have a dog. It's not fair to him." But how could she possibly resist those eyes? she thought.

"What if you didn't need to work all day? Or what if you could bring your dog to work?"

"MD would never go for that," she said, giving a short laugh at the idea.

"I would," he said. "You could come to work for me. I'd double your salary."

Emma dropped her jaw.

"Or," he said, carefully watching her. "You could put me out of my misery and marry me."

Emma's head was spinning. It took her a full moment to find her voice. "Misery?" she said.

He stepped closer and slid his fingers through her hair, tilting her head so that she could see his face, the ruthless scar and dark gaze full of passion and something far deeper. "I've been missing a home most of my life. Being with you makes me feel like I finally found where I belong."

Emma's knees weakened and she felt her eyes well with tears. "Oh, Damien," she whispered. "I never thought this was possible. I never thought you would let me into your heart."

"Trust me, woman. You're in," he said in a rough voice.

Emma saw the love shining in his eyes and felt as if she needed to pinch herself.

"You think you can go the distance with me? You turned me away before."

Emma shook her head. "I was afraid of how much I felt for you. And then you told me to leave."

"That was pure hell. I didn't want you to stay because I was forcing you."

She studied his face. "And part of the reason you decided not to go after Max—"

"Was you," he finished for her. "It just didn't seem as important anymore."

Emma shook her head. "We've both made mistakes."

He took a deep breath and expelled it, looking away from her. "I thought you hated me."

"I thought I should," she said, feeling a deep stab of pain even as she said the words. "I hated myself for trying to deceive you."

"I understood."

Emma felt her throat knot and her eyes sting with unshed tears. If he'd come back after she'd turned him away, then she needed to bare her heart to him. It was only fair. "You're an amazing man. I don't know when it happened, but somewhere along the line, you became my soulmate, my rescuer. Somewhere along the line you made me belong to you."

His nostrils flared as he drew in another breath. "Amazing, huh. Amazing enough for you to marry?"

Her heart stopped. "Do you love me?"

He closed his eyes for a moment and her heart seemed to sink into the floor.

"I don't know much about love, but I know I

love you. More than my life. More than I ever thought possible."

Emma couldn't hold back the tears any longer. "Oh, Damien." She slid her arms around the back of his neck, craving his closeness. "We could have given up on each other. The thought of it terrifies me."

"It wouldn't have happened. If I couldn't convince you, then I hoped the dog would." His gaze turned serious. "More than anything, I wanted to hear you say you believe in me."

"I do," she said, lifting her hand to his cheek. "I'll believe in you for the rest of our lives."

Damien pulled her off her feet against him. "And I love you. Lord, you feel good. How do you feel about getting married in Vegas?"

She smiled, feeling giddy. "Anywhere is good."

"And how do you feel about a honeymoon in Italy?"

She drew back slightly to look into his face. His lips turned up at the edges and his eyes glinted with happiness. "I talked with Max. He did some research into the dirty deal his grandfather did with mine and he has set aside a cottage for the Medici family forever."

Stunned, she stared at him. "You're kidding."

He shook his head. "He's a stand-up guy just like you said."

"You're the most stand-up guy I've ever met," she said, thinking of how many times he had already come through for her. She was the luckiest woman in the world.

"I love you," he said simply. "And I'll spend the rest of my life making your wishes come true."

"I love you, too." She knew, with all her heart, that he was telling the truth. She also knew, with all her heart, that her biggest wish had just come true.

* * * * *

*In honor of our 60th anniversary, Harlequin®
American Romance® is celebrating by featuring
an all-American male each month,
all year long with*
MEN MADE IN AMERICA!
*This June, we'll be featuring American men
living in the West.*

Here's a sneak preview of
THE CHIEF RANGER by Rebecca Winters.

*Chief Ranger Vance Rossiter has to confront the
sister of a man who died while under Vance's
watch…and also confront his attraction to her.*

"Chief Ranger Rossiter?" The sight of the woman who'd stepped inside Vance's office brought him to his feet. "I'm Rachel Darrow. Your secretary said I should come right in."

"Please," he said, walking around his desk to shake her hand. At a glance he estimated she was in her mid-twenties. Her feminine curves did wonders for the pale blue T-shirt and jeans she was wearing. "Ranger Jarvis informed me there's a young boy with you."

The unfriendly expression in her beautiful green eyes caught him off guard. "Yes," was her clipped reply. "When we arrived in Yosemite the ranger told me I couldn't go anywhere in the park until I talked to you first."

"That's right."

"Knowing you wanted this meeting to be private, he offered to show my nephew around Headquarters."

So this woman was the victim's sister.... "What's his name?"

"Nicky."

The boy who haunted Vance's dreams now had a name. "How old is he?"

"He turned six three weeks ago. Were you the man in charge when my brother and sister-in-law were killed?"

"Yes. To tell you I'm sorry for what happened couldn't begin to convey my feelings."

The woman's gaze didn't flicker. "I won't even try to describe mine. Just tell me one thing. Was their accident preventable?"

"Yes," he answered without hesitation.

"In other words, the people working under you fell asleep on your watch and two lives were snuffed out as a result."

Hearing it put like that, he had to set the record straight. "My staff had nothing to do with it. I, myself, could have prevented the loss of life."

Ms. Darrow's expression hardened. "So you admit culpability."

"Yes. I take full blame."

A look of pain crossed over her features. "You can just stand there and admit it?" Her cry echoed that of his own tortured soul.

"Yes." He sucked in his breath.

"I work for a cruise line. Aboard ship, it's the captain's responsibility to maintain rigid safety regulations. If a disaster like that had happened while he was in charge he would have been relieved of his command and never given another ship again."

Rachel Darrow couldn't know she was preaching to the converted. "If you've come to the park with the intention of bringing a lawsuit against me for negligence, maybe you should." It would only be what he deserved.

"Maybe I will."

In the next instant, she wheeled around and hurried out of his office. Vance could have gone after her, but it would cause a scene, something he was loath to do for a variety of reasons. In the first place, he needed to cool down before he approached her again.

The discovery of the Darrows' frozen bodies had affected every ranger in the park. A little boy had been orphaned—a boy whose aunt was all he had left.

* * * * *

*Will Rachel allow Vance to explain—and will
she let him into her heart?
Find out in
THE CHIEF RANGER
Available June 2009 from
Harlequin® American Romance®.*

We'll be spotlighting a different series every month throughout 2009 to celebrate our 60th anniversary.

Look for Harlequin® American Romance® in June!

Join us for a year-long celebration of the rugged American male! From cops to cowboys— Men Made in America has the hero you've been dreaming about!

Look for

The Chief Ranger

by Rebecca Winters, on sale in June!

www.eHarlequin.com　　　　　HARBPA09

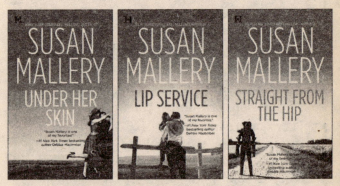

You're invited to join our Tell Harlequin Reader Panel!

By joining our new reader panel you will:

- Receive Harlequin® books—they are FREE and yours to keep with no obligation to purchase anything!
- Participate in fun online surveys
- Exchange opinions and ideas with women just like you
- Have a say in our new book ideas and help us publish the best in women's fiction

In addition, you will have a chance to win great prizes and receive special gifts!
See Web site for details. Some conditions apply.
Space is limited.

To join, visit us at
www.TellHarlequin.com.

Tell HARLEQUIN

REQUEST YOUR FREE BOOKS!

2 FREE NOVELS PLUS 2 FREE GIFTS!

Silhouette® Desire®

Passionate, Powerful, Provocative!

Do you crave dark and sensual paranormal tales?

Get your fix with Silhouette Nocturne!

In print:
Two new titles available every month wherever books are sold.

Online:
Nocturne eBooks available monthly from **www.silhouettenocturne.com.**

Nocturne Bites:
Short sensual paranormal stories available monthly online from **www.nocturnebites.com** and in print with the Nocturne Bites collections available April 2009 and October 2009 wherever books are sold.

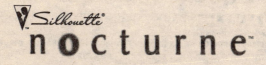

www.silhouettenocturne.com
www.paranormalromanceblog.com

Silhouette Desire

COMING NEXT MONTH
Available June 9, 2009

#1945 THE BRIDE HUNTER—Ann Major
Man of the Month
When he finally locates his runaway bride, he discovers she's been keeping more than a few secrets from him...like the fact that he's a father!

#1946 SEDUCED INTO A PAPER MARRIAGE—Maureen Child
The Hudsons of Beverly Hills
No one has ever crossed him—until his wife of convenience walks out on him. Determined to present a united front at the Oscars, he sets out to reclaim his wife...and their marriage bed.

#1947 WYOMING WEDDING—Sara Orwig
Stetsons & CEOs
His first love has always been money, so when this billionaire marries to get ahead in business, he's completely unprepared for the sparks that fly!

#1948 THE PRODIGAL PRINCE'S SEDUCTION—Olivia Gates
The Castaldini Crown
The prince has no idea his new lover has come to him with ulterior motives. But when he proposes marriage, will he discover what she's really after?

#1949 VALENTE'S BABY—Maxine Sullivan
Billionaires and Babies
A one-night stand results in a tiny Valente heir. Can this playboy commit to more than just giving his baby his name?

#1950 BEDDED BY BLACKMAIL—Robyn Grady
His suddenly gorgeous housekeeper is about to move on—until he discovers the sizzling passion they share under the covers. Now he'll stop at nothing to keep her there.

SDCNMBPA0509

PUT YOURSELF IN THE PICTURE!

Enter the SWEET DREAMS® Cover Girl Contest and see yourself on the cover of a SWEET DREAMS book!

If you've ever dreamed of becoming a model and seeing your face gazing from the covers of books all across America, this is the contest for you!

Girls from age 11 to 16 are eligible. Just fill out the coupon below and send it in, along with two photographs of yourself (one close-up and one full length standing pose)* and an essay telling why you enjoy SWEET DREAMS books. The Grand Prize Winner will be chosen by an expert panel of judges—including a beauty editor from *Young Miss* magazine!

The Grand Prize is a trip to New York City for you and your chaperone, where you will be photographed for the cover of an upcoming SWEET DREAMS novel! The Grand Prize Winner will also receive a complete professional makeover, have an interview at a top modeling agency and enjoy a dinner date with a SWEET DREAMS author!

Five lucky Second Prize Winners will receive make-up kits!

So don't delay—enter the contest today!

*Photographs must have been taken within 6 months of contest entry.

SWEET DREAMS Cover Girl Contest
Bantam Books, Inc.
Dept. NP
666 Fifth Avenue
New York, NY 10103

Name_____ Age_____

Address_____

City _____ State _____ Zip _____

No purchase necessary. All entries must be received no later than December 31, 1985. The winners will be announced and notified by January 31, 1986. Chances of winning depend on number of entrants.

Employees of Bantam Books, Inc., their subsidiaries and affiliates, and their immediate families, are not eligible to enter. This contest is void where prohibited by law. Not available to residents of Quebec. All Federal, State and Local regulations apply. By entering, entrants agree to the use without charge of their name, address and likeness for publicity purposes. No photographs submitted will be returned. Bantam Books is not responsible for entries lost, misdirected or delayed in the mail.

Exp. 12/31/85   C17—9/85

death. And Elizabeth understood now how vital it was for her brother to begin to pick up the pieces of his life. He just couldn't go on forever remembering the past, she thought, her heart aching for her brother. Sooner or later he had to take a deep breath and begin to look forward again. And from what Lila reported, it sounded as though Steven had made a tentative move in that direction that night.

But Betsy Martin had made certain his guilt would snuff out the first sparks of interest he felt for Cara Walker.

How dare she, Elizabeth thought furiously, *after everything Steve did to help her after Tricia's death? Doesn't she realize it's time for him to set himself free from mourning?*

God, I hope Steve can let himself go and begin a new life! And I hope Betsy Martin has the decency to step back and let him find happiness after all these months!

Will Betsy Martin stand in the way of Steven and Cara's happiness? Find out in Sweet Valley High #24, **MEMORIES.**

anxious expression on Jessica's pretty face. "She called to find out if you were OK."

"Is that all she said?" Elizabeth asked, wondering if the look on her sister's face had anything to do with Steven's strange behavior.

Jessica shook her head. "Poor Steve," she murmured. "It sounds like Betsy Martin really gave him a hard time tonight."

"What do you mean?" Elizabeth asked, her curiosity rising.

Jessica shrugged. "Well, I guess I was right about Steve and Cara. Lila said as soon as I left they started dancing together—slow dances—and they were attracting a little bit of attention. She said it looked like they were acting pretty crazy about each other."

"And—" Elizabeth prompted.

"And Betsy Martin came up to them on the dance floor and made a real scene. Lila said she was incredibly nasty. She said something like, 'Don't you think it's a little soon for that sort of behavior? Or have you forgotten my sister already?' And Lila said Steve went pale, and his eyes filled up with tears. He stormed off the dance floor and left without even saying good night to poor Cara."

"Oh, no," Elizabeth moaned, putting her face in her hands. Poor, poor Steven! If he *had* been having a good time with Cara, he certainly deserved it. It had been months since Tricia's need to grow by meeting new people. And after that, all we can do is wait and see."

Steven let out a low whistle. "Boy, you guys really did some talking tonight! Is Nicholas OK?" he asked gently.

"I think so." Elizabeth sighed. "Boy, have I ever learned my lesson," she added. "I just wasn't ready for that sort of thing at all. I know I hurt Nicholas, but I think he'll be all right. And I think he knew what he was getting into anyway. Maybe one day we'll be able to be real friends."

"I bet you will," Steven said softly.

"I hate to change the subject," Jessica piped up, "but I couldn't help noticing how much time you spent with Cara Walker tonight. I don't suppose you changed your mind about her?"

Steven's expression darkened. "I don't want to talk about that," he said angrily, pushing his chair back and getting up from the table. "I'm glad you're OK, Liz," he called behind him as he stomped out of the room.

Elizabeth stared at her sister. "I think you hit a nerve. But I wonder how? He sure seems tense about something!"

Her question was cut off by the telephone, its unexpected ring shattering the late-night silence.

"I'll get it," Jessica said, leaping for the receiver before the second ring.

"It was Lila," she reported several minutes later, turning to face her sister. There was an

"What luck!" Steven said, coming into the kitchen and rumpling first Jessica's hair and then Elizabeth's. "Both my sisters in one shot. This must be my lucky night."

You see, Jessica's expression said plainly to her sister. Something was up. Steven's cheerfulness seemed forced.

"I've been worried about you," Steven said to Elizabeth, dropping into a chair next to her and studying her face. "Were you all right tonight? What happened?"

"Everything's fine now," Elizabeth said, her face glowing. "I found Todd, and we were able to talk the whole thing out. First of all . . ." She backed up, seeing the puzzled expression on her brother's face. "I explained to Nicholas that I'm just not ready for any serious involvement. I still feel too much for Todd. I know I need to date, and I think in time . . ."

Steven watched his sister quietly, the warmth in his eyes showing her how glad he was to hear what she was saying.

"Well, to make a long story short, Todd and I agreed to leave everything very open-ended. We're going to see each other as much as we can without interfering with each other's lives. And we'll call from time to time, and certainly write letters. But we both see now that we can't limit ourselves to long-distance love, either. We both

150

this time, Jessica thought sadly. *And my twin had to foul everything up. And for what—the chance to see the thoroughly mediocre Todd Wilkins every couple of months?*

In the second place, she'd gotten absolutely nowhere at the dating agency. What a waste that place was, she thought moodily. Spence Millgate was nothing but a complete nerd. And from what Elizabeth had told her, it didn't sound as if the women she'd found for Steven were much better.

"Hey," she said suddenly, sitting up straight in her chair. She had just remembered what Betsy Martin had said to her earlier in the evening. "You're going to think this sounds really stupid, Liz, but I have a feeling Steve's up to something tonight."

Elizabeth wrinkled her nose. "Up to something? What are you talking about, Jess?"

"He was being really friendly to Cara tonight," Jessica told her. "I know, I know. You don't believe me. But it's true, Liz. I wouldn't have thought anything of it myself. But I happened to bump into Betsy Martin, and she was absolutely livid about the whole thing. She was ready to go on the rampage, right then and there. Only—"

"I didn't know Betsy was there tonight," Elizabeth said, looking slightly more interested.

"Ssshh!" she admonished. "I think I hear Steve now."

unless he asks for your help, you have no right forcing women on him."

"Was Jody MacGuire really foul?" Jessica asked, a giggle in her voice.

Elizabeth relaxed into laughter, despite herself. "Completely foul. Almost as bad as that guy you were with tonight. What was his name?"

"Spence Millgate." Jessica groaned. "Don't worry, Liz. I'm definitely retiring from the matchmaking business. On Monday I'm giving my notice at the agency, and from then on . . ."

Elizabeth's eyes narrowed as she looked at her twin. "If I didn't know better, Jess, I'd almost suspect you of having something to do with Nicholas Morrow's revived interest in me!"

Jessica's eyes widened innocently. "I can't believe you, Liz," she said sadly. "My own flesh and blood . . . and do you trust me, even the tiniest little bit? It's pathetic!"

Elizabeth looked closely at her twin, then burst out laughing. "Don't give me that innocent look," she warned. "After tonight, Jess, as far as I'm concerned, you're capable of anything!"

What a mess, Jessica thought. In the first place, she'd probably made a permanent enemy of Nicholas. From what Elizabeth had said, it sounded as if Nicholas was never even going to talk to her again. And if he was irritated with Elizabeth, he was bound to be good and ticked off at Jessica. *I promised him things would work out*

148

Fourteen

"Hey, I wonder what's keeping Steve," Jessica said, obviously trying to change the subject. "It's after midnight, and he still isn't back from Lila's. Do you think—"

"Steve," Elizabeth pointed out as they sat in the kitchen, "is just another reason for you to apologize, Jessica Wakefield. What's this business of using the computer at work to fix him up with people? Don't you think that's kind of lousy?"

"I didn't use the computer," Jessica pointed out. "For goodness sake, Liz. All I was doing was trying to help him out. I mean, look at the guy! He never has a date, never talks to a single girl, other than you or me. And—"

"That's beside the point," Elizabeth snapped. "What Steve does is his own business. And